O9-BHJ-205

A Convenient Amish Bride

Lucy Bayer

LOVE INSPIRED
INSPIRATIONAL ROMANCE

LOVE INSPIRED®
INSPIRATIONAL ROMANCE

Recycling programs
for this product may
not exist in your area.

ISBN-13: 978-1-335-58657-5

A Convenient Amish Bride

Love Inspired
22 Adelaide St. West, 41st Floor
Toronto, Ontario M5H 4E3, Canada
www.LoveInspired.com

Printed in U.S.A.

"We could get married."

Ruby's cheeks burned as David stared at her, not open-mouthed with shock, but close.

"Walk to my buggy with me," he murmured.

She barely heard him over the pounding of her heart in her ears. Had she really said that? What must he think of her? "I've grown fond of the girls," she said when he still didn't say anything. "I don't think Mindy would be opposed to the idea."

"I was thinking of hiring a nanny," he said. "If you quit your job at the restaurant, I could pay you—"

She was aware of the skin of her face, stretched too tight over her bones. "That would mean trading one job for another. And…and then I'd have to find something else if you married one day."

He shook his head, his eyes unhappy. "I don't want to marry again. I don't want to get married at all."

Oh.

"I don't—" He exhaled noisily. "You surprised me. I'm not saying no."

He *wasn't*?

Lucy Bayer writes Amish novels from her home in the Midwest. She is a mother of four and an avid birder.

Books by Lucy Bayer

Love Inspired

A Convenient Amish Bride

Visit the Author Profile page at LoveInspired.com.

A threefold cord is not quickly broken.
—*Ecclesiastes* 4:12

Chapter One

"**R**uby is quiet again today."

"Do you think she's ill?"

Ruby Kaufmann stood in a small nook in the bustling Amish restaurant out of sight of the two young women speaking in hushed tones. She didn't have to see them to know it was Emma Yoder and Naomi King speaking. She'd been working at the restaurant for weeks now, and she recognized their voices above the sound of tinkling silverware. There was no rustle of their dresses as if they were walking. It was the lull before the supper rush. They must be wrapping silverware into paper napkins, one of the many small jobs in a restaurant like this.

"I think Jonah Schrock was seated in her section again during lunch. Everyone knows he's looking for a wife."

"How convenient. Ruby needs a husband."

Her cheeks burned. This wasn't the first time she'd overheard the two girls talking about her. Emma and Naomi had been hired on a few weeks ago, both on the same day. Ruby had worked at the restaurant in Hickory Harbor, Ohio, for nearly two years. And she was a curiosity. Most girls her age—twenty-four—were married, and some had started their families.

She didn't rush out of the alcove and confront them. She kept her head down as she refilled the small caddies with packets of sugar. She could do that by touch when her eyes filled with tears that had to be blinked back.

Ruby needs a husband.

Emma and Naomi couldn't know how their flippant comment brought back the old ache. Like a broken bone that had never healed correctly. They didn't know about Jonathan—Ruby's perfect match who had passed away years ago. Or the family dinner from just yesterday, where Ruby's brother Evan had delivered news that had been a reminder of everything she would never have.

"What Ruby needs is friends who aren't busybodies."

Ruby's head came up at the third voice. Lovina Fisher was the head waitress at this restaurant—the only waitress who'd worked there longer than Ruby. Her family had run the business for twenty years, and she'd grown up in the kitchen. She was older than Ruby by five or so years.

Ruby and Lovina had become close friends. They had outlasted all the other waitresses, who seemed to work in the restaurant for a few months before they got married.

Lovina murmured something Ruby couldn't make out. She heard the swishing of long skirts and aprons before all three women came round the alcove corner.

"We were only teasing a bit," Naomi said, her voice a hint breathless.

"Sorry." Emma seemed even more abashed, her head ducked so that Ruby had more of a view of her prayer *kapp* than her face.

"It's okay." Ruby said the words when she didn't really feel them. The speculation happened more frequently than she would've liked. Every few months when a new waitress started. She rarely heard any gossip about Lovina, likely because of her connection to the restaurant. Nobody wanted to risk their job gossiping about the owner's daughter.

Ruby said what she'd begun to say whenever this came up. "I don't want a husband." She swallowed a tight knot that rose in her throat, because that wasn't strictly the truth. She had always wanted a husband and family. She just wouldn't have one.

Emma and Naomi exchanged a confused look for a split second. They didn't seem to know what to say to that. They were seventeen and nineteen, respectively, and she doubted either one of them had experienced tragedy. There was an innocence about them that said the world was full of goodness and light. Their lives stretched ahead of them with unlimited hope. Husbands, homes, children, a long life of happiness.

Ruby's happiness had been cut short.

Lovina shooed the other girls back to work, this time to the front of the restaurant to stock the shelves with the jams, jellies and other goodies the family made in the restaurant kitchen.

Lovina joined Ruby at the small worktable in the alcove. She reached for an empty sugar caddy and began counting out the packets to put inside. "Are you all right?"

"*Ja.* Of course." Ruby *should* be used to the speculation. What had happened to Jonathan was so long ago. She'd been fourteen when he had died. Only she and *Mamm* had known he was her special match.

"They can't understand."

As their friendship had deepened, Ruby couldn't help noticing that Lovina never pried. Not about Jonathan. Lovina's ability to shut down gossip had given Ruby the courage to open up about her loss. *Mamm* had passed away within a year after Jonathan's death. Long before Ruby had come out of her grief enough to wonder whether she might have a different match, *Mamm* was gone.

"No, I suppose not. But it's nice that you do," Ruby said. "We'll be working here together until we're old and gray."

Lovina chuckled.

She'd never asked Lovina about her past. But there had to be some reason why her friend was unmarried at almost thirty. It wasn't something they talked about.

"My brother and his wife are expecting," Ruby said. There was a sort of relief saying the words.

Lovina kept her gaze on the sugar packets and the caddy at her fingertips. "Which one?"

Ruby had three brothers. Two older and one younger. "Evan and Beth. They told everyone at supper last night."

She'd started out the night content with *oohing* and *aahing* over her young niece Hannah's watercolor paintings. She adored her niece and four nephews. Both her older brothers and their wives had started their families soon after they married.

She'd been holding eleven-month-old Benjamin, rocking him to sleep when Evan had made the announcement. Beth's shy nature had kept her seated with a rosy blush on her face as everyone around the long wooden table had shared excited congratulations.

Ruby had hid a jolt of grief by snuggling the baby.

I don't want a husband.

The trouble was, she did want a husband and a family. But she shouldn't want that.

And today, overhearing Emma and Naomi made her grief more poignant.

Lovina understood. She kept up a stream of small talk that gave Ruby time to breathe through the grief of losing *Mamm*, a long-ago hurt never quite healed that she often thought about when Jonathan came up. And the grief she *shouldn't* feel after so long. A pinch of jealousy over what Evan and Beth had.

It wasn't long before the dining room tables filled up. As usual, it was a mixture of *Englishers* and Amish folk. One table held a college-age couple who didn't look up from their phones when Ruby arrived at the table. At another sat a couple roughly the age of Ruby's parents, and for a moment when she dropped off their meals, she felt a wave of missing her *mamm*.

Ruby filled two coffee cups and still had the carafe in hand when she approached an Amish family that had just been seated in her section.

A man with dark hair and beard, dressed in a hand-sewn linen shirt and trousers. A tiny girl—

she couldn't be older than eighteen months—sat on his knee, and a second little girl of about four sat across from him. Both girls wore matching pink dresses and black shoes. The man's head was bent as he said something to the girl on his knee.

Where was his wife? Perhaps she had ducked into the restroom?

Ruby came even with the table at the same moment his profile came into view. Recognition flared. David Weiss.

David was a handsome farrier, well known around Hickory Harbor. She often saw him at house-church, though she'd never spoken to him before today.

He was a widower. There was no wife in the restroom or anywhere else.

"Hello. *Denke* for coming in tonight. I'm Ruby. Can I get you something to drink?"

David glanced up, and she saw faint recognition flair in his expression. "Hello." His head tilted slightly. "Are you… Noah's daughter?"

She nodded.

His expression eased into a tired smile. "I was out at the dairy shoeing his big bay only a couple of weeks ago. How is he?"

"*Goot.* I'll be sure to tell him you said hello."

She filled the water cups at the table from the

pitcher, moving both cup and pitcher with deft hands when the littlest girl reached for it.

"You have *goot* reflexes," David said.

"I have a niece and nephews." She finished filling the last glass. "And I've worked here for a while."

Surprise flashed across his expression. "You don't help out with the dairy, then?"

She wrinkled her nose. "Cows are too big and smelly, don't you think?" She directed her question to the little girl sitting across from him, so serious and silent.

She won a tentative smile, though the girl quickly looked down at her doll.

When Ruby glanced back to David, she found his gaze on her face. Heat pricked her cheeks as he stared at her, unspeaking.

The little girl on his lap babbled a string of nonsense words Ruby didn't understand.

David's attention was diverted, his stare finally falling away. He smiled at the girl across the table. "Mindy loves cows. And horses. Don't you?"

Mindy nodded gravely. She didn't speak, but her serious brown eyes darted around, watching everything around her.

Ruby waited a moment too long, and when the silence stretched, she cleared her throat. "Do you know what you'd like to order?"

* * *

David was surprised by his reaction to the pretty waitress. Ruby. For a moment there, he hadn't been able to look away from her.

He didn't have time to stay surprised as Maggie wiggled on his lap, banging her tiny fists on the table.

Ruby disappeared into the restaurant kitchen, and he was left with his girls.

"Did you have a good day with *Grossmammi*?" he asked.

Maggie beamed up at him, babbling happy words like *duck* and *house* and *dog*.

Mindy sat across from them listening and watching.

What would it take to get her to speak to him? Just one word, and he'd know he wasn't failing as a father.

She hadn't spoken since her *mamm* had passed away nine months ago. He remembered when she was Maggie's age and talked until she had to stop to catch her breath. To him. To her dolls. To her *mamm*. Mindy was a chatterbox.

Or at least she used to be. What did she do with all the words she kept inside? After so long, he was at a loss for how to comfort her. He'd solicited help from the bishop of their church. The local doctor, a family practitioner, had advised that there wasn't anything physically wrong with her and that she'd speak when she was ready.

How could David help her when he couldn't even help himself?

"What about you, Mindy? Did you have a good day?"

She nodded gravely. She looked down to stroke the doll in her lap.

His *mamm* thought Mindy would grow out of it. He prayed for that every night.

He was blessed to have his parents' help now that Jessica was gone. He had no one else.

Unlike many other large Amish families, it had just been the three of them.

His parents had been older when he had been born. He must've been about Mindy's age when he'd asked why he couldn't have a brother to play with.

Daed's expression had crumpled, and he'd looked away, but not before he'd told David never to ask that again.

David hadn't.

If he had brothers and sisters, maybe someone else would be able to help.

He felt as if he were drowning.

Three months ago, he'd moved closer to his parents, uprooting the girls from the home they had been born in.

He'd made a successful career as a farrier. It

was a job that was far too dangerous to bring the girls along with him. It would take only an instant of not watching them for a horse to step on one of them. Or the other innumerable dangerous situations they could get into on an Amish farm.

They wouldn't be old enough for school for several years. He'd struggled for months after Jessica's death, but it came down to the fact that he needed someone to watch them while he worked.

When a small house near his parents had come up for sale, he'd bought it and moved the girls. Now *Mamm* watched them while he was away for the day.

What he hadn't been prepared for was seeing how much his parents had slowed down over the past years. He'd been so busy with his growing family and his business that he hadn't noticed the changes.

When he'd been a boy, his *mamm* kept her kitchen spotless. Today, when he had arrived to pick up the girls after work, dishes from lunch and breakfast were still in the sink.

Dinner hadn't been started, even though his stomach had grumbled with hunger. He'd quickly washed the dishes, but his mother had shooed him out of the kitchen when he offered to cook. She'd clucked about leftovers in the fridge, and

David was so tired he hadn't wanted to argue with her.

He'd stopped by his *daed's* workshop, tamping down the usual frustration he felt when his father barely looked up from the piece he was working on.

"Does she need to see a doctor?" David had asked earlier.

"What for? We're both getting older. She just gets tired more easily than she used to." *Daed's* answer had not satisfied him, especially not when he added, "She loves the girls, but they can be a handful."

David knew how much energy the girls expended every day. They were active and curious and playful. Just last week, Mindy had snuck away from *Mamm* and walked down the street to a neighbor's house to see their baby chicks. *Mamm* hadn't noticed until the young man had brought Mindy home.

Was *Daed* right? Was David worrying when he didn't need to?

He wasn't convinced.

Tonight he and the girls had stopped at the restaurant out of convenience and hunger. There was no one waiting at home to cook for them. Only laundry. Enough of it to keep him up late tonight.

Was *Mamm* behind on laundry, too?

The waitress was back, placing small glasses of milk on the table for the girls, along with the lemonade he had ordered.

Ruby looked tired. She had violet circles under her eyes, and she carried tension in her shoulders. There was something about her that seemed… lonely.

Maggie reached her arms toward Ruby.

He shook his head. "No, *Dochder*. Ruby is working."

Ruby smiled, and heat rushed into his cheeks. What was wrong with him tonight?

He opened his mouth, not sure what he meant to say, but she was already gone, bussing another table across the restaurant.

Maggie reached for the silverware, and he quickly scooted it farther away from her grabby hands.

Jessica would be ashamed of him. His late wife had been a gentle soul, and he'd loved her deeply. He shouldn't even be noticing another, not when he was still grieving. Some days he was fine. He worked and took care of the house and did everything that needed to be done and almost felt happy. Almost.

Some days, he didn't want to get out of bed for missing Jessica.

Ruby returned to the table, this time with her arms laden with their food. She placed his pot pie in front of him, careful that it was far enough back so that Maggie wouldn't be able to reach it. Ruby put the toasted cheese sandwich in front of Mindy and a second one in front of Maggie. Mindy's glass was nearly empty.

"Would you like some more water?"

Mindy shook her head slightly.

"Are you sure?" Ruby had started to lean toward Mindy but now recoiled. "Is that a—?" Ruby looked frantically at David.

He had no idea what had startled her, but he carefully sat Maggie beside him on the inside of the booth.

"What?"

Mindy was clutching her doll to her chest. It was wiggling.

Because it wasn't a doll at all, but Mindy's rabbit with blond-colored fur.

"We don't allow animals in the restaurant," Ruby whispered. Thankfully she had kept her voice down, or the other patrons might have overheard and gotten upset.

"I know that. Mindy, give me the rabbit."

Mindy's lips pressed together stubbornly. His heart leaped.

Would she argue with him?

For a split second, he fervently wished for it. An argumentative daughter was better than a silent one.

But she handed him the bunny wrapped in a doll's dress, which was entirely the wrong shape for the furry body.

His food was on the table, and his stomach grumbled loudly enough for Ruby to hear.

"I don't suppose you have a box or a crate? I'll take her out to the buggy, but I don't want her to get loose or get hurt."

Ruby pointed toward the front of the restaurant. "We were unloading some jams and jellies earlier. There might be a box left over."

"Would you watch the girls for just a second?"

She nodded, her wide eyes staring at the bundle of wiggling rabbit in his hands.

It took longer than he wanted to find an empty box tucked behind the hostess counter and deposit the rabbit in his buggy.

When he returned out of breath from hurrying and worried that Ruby might've abandoned his daughters—it wasn't her job to watch them, and she had other customers—he found her sitting at the table with Maggie standing on the seat behind her, leaning on Ruby's shoulder. Mindy sat listening raptly as Ruby spoke.

Ruby saw him approaching and stood, steadying Maggie before she toppled out of the booth after her.

David came even with Ruby. "Thanks," he murmured.

"Why a rabbit?" she whispered.

He shrugged. "Because she's four? She loves animals." This close, he could see the splash of freckles across the bridge of her nose when it wrinkled.

"But where did she get it?"

"From home. I'm sorry I didn't notice."

He'd been distracted by worries for his *mamm* and his hungry stomach. It rumbled again now, and Ruby scooted out of his way.

Her shoulder brushed against his arm, and he got a whiff of some sweet-smelling soap. He exhaled noisily as he sat back down. He wasn't hungry anymore.

He was still failing his daughters, and he didn't know what to do about it.

Chapter Two

On the weekends, the restaurant rented a booth at the local farmers market, where the staff sold its wares. Jams, jellies, packaged cinnamon rolls and sweet rolls. It was a rotating schedule, and today Ruby was working with Lovina.

They'd both been up since before sunrise, riding in Lovina's family buggy the four miles to the fairgrounds where the market was held.

The sun was shining, and the early autumn breeze had only a hint of chill to it. Ruby had shrugged out of her shawl by midmorning.

"She offered what?" Lovina was restocking a stack of strawberry jam from a box beneath the table.

"Lily brought it up two other times," Ruby murmured from her spot, standing and smiling at customers. Their booth was empty for the moment. "My sister-in-law wants me to act like a nanny. But an unpaid one. She said I could quit my job."

Lovina harrumphed, and Ruby felt vindicated. She'd needed to tell someone about *Daed's* decision to move into the *daadi haus*, about Lily asking her to be a nanny.

Ruby had been unsettled since the moment it had happened one morning last week as she'd been pushing her bike out to the street to head to work.

She took a moment to wave at the man in the booth across the wide outdoor aisle. He must be at least two years older than her, which would make him about Lovina's age. He was from a neighboring Amish community. Since they saw him every other Saturday, and he'd helped them with their tables once, they'd formed a casual friendship.

"I'd rather get an apartment on my own than be stuck in a house with Lily all day long." Ruby looked up, saw Lovina's raised eyebrows and realized the words were true even as she said them.

Ruby mulled over her words as Lovina handed two jars of pear preserves to an *Englisher* woman in exchange for the ten-dollar bill she extended over the table.

When the woman left, Ruby said, "Maybe I *should* look for an apartment." She had known that her father would one day move into the *daadi haus*, but she hadn't expected it to happen now. *Daed* had suggested it after Evan and Beth's announcement about the baby.

Ruby wasn't ready to leave the home she'd been born in, even to move across the yard. But neither was she willing to be a nanny for Lily. They'd annoy each other too much.

"What would your *daed* say?"

"I don't know," Ruby murmured. "Maybe I could make a case for living closer to the restaurant."

Lovina ducked behind the table to unbox several more jars of preserves. "You said something last week that I haven't been able to get out of my mind. About us working at the restaurant together for a long time into the future."

Ruby greeted an Amish couple and sold them a box of cinnamon rolls before Lovina continued the conversation.

"When you first started at the restaurant, I thought you were like all the other girls—just passing time until you met someone and married. But then we became friends."

Ruby smiled. "What are you saying? You want to get an apartment together?"

"Maybe."

Their booth got busy, and Ruby considered the idea. She knew Lovina still lived with her parents. She hadn't known her friend was considering a change.

Before the next customer approached, Ruby saw the cloth covering the candlemaker's table twitching. Had something crawled underneath? A cat or dog maybe?

She was distracted by a couple of familiar faces and waved to an *Englisher* couple who visited the restaurant regularly.

Her gaze was drawn to the tablecloth again. This time she saw the tip of a tiny black shoe sticking out from beneath it.

The candlemaker had been alone all morning. There'd been no sign of a younger sibling with him.

So who was hiding under the table?

The breeze quieted, and for a moment, the throngs of people had emptied from between the two booths. In the sudden stillness, Ruby thought she heard a soft sob.

Curiosity compelled her out of the booth. She told Lovina she would be right back.

Her friend's curious gaze followed her.

The candlemaker was speaking to an *Englisher* couple, and he caught sight of her as she crossed the grassy space between their booths. His eyes widened, and he started to smile, but his expression faltered as she moved toward the opposite corner of his booth from where he stood.

Then she lost sight of him as she bent down. She gently lifted the corner of the tablecloth. Surprise coursed through her as she caught sight of David Weiss's oldest girl. The little one's face was wet from tears and smudged with dirt as if she'd been wiping her cheeks with grubby hands. She looked at Ruby with wide, fearful eyes.

Compassion stirred in Ruby. Something was clearly wrong.

She slowly knelt in the grass, not caring if her skirt got dirty. She laid her hands on both her knees so the girl could see them and know she wasn't a threat.

"Do you remember me? From the restaurant a few days ago? My name is Ruby."

The girl's brow wrinkled, and then her expression cleared as she nodded slowly.

That night, Ruby had watched over their table with more attentiveness than was strictly necessary, and she couldn't remember seeing the serious little girl speak once.

She'd nodded in response to Ruby's question. Obviously, she could hear and understand. Did she have a disability that kept her mute? Or was it simply her choice not to speak?

Ruby craned her neck to look around, all without moving from her spot next to the girl. She didn't see David's broad-shouldered figure anywhere. She had known his parents when she was a teenager and looked for them, too.

They weren't in sight.

There was no frantic movement in the crowd, no one calling out for a little girl.

But that didn't mean David wasn't looking. He might be farther away.

He had seemed a conscientious father the other night. He must be worried about his little girl.

"Is your *daed* here?" she asked softly.

The little girl nodded.

She wasn't outright crying, but Ruby knew the girl was still on the verge of tears.

"Did you get separated?"

Another small nod, this one accompanied by the swell of new tears.

What Ruby needed was a distraction to keep the girl calm.

She pointed over her shoulder to Lovina in their booth. Her friend was watching her even as she spoke to a man in a T-shirt and jeans.

"That's my friend Miss Lovina from the restaurant. We are serving cinnamon rolls and other goodies this morning. I know your *daed* will be looking for you. Do you want to come over and sit with us and have a cinnamon roll while we wait for him to come?"

The girl's eyes brightened infinitesimally. She put her thumb in her mouth.

Ruby tried not to wince at how dirty the digit was. The girl was probably too old for such a thing, but Ruby knew she must be frightened and overwhelmed.

Ruby held out her hand. After a moment's hesitation, the girl put her small hand into Ruby's larger one. She felt a stirring of something both sorrowful and hopeful. She ignored it with all her might as she stood up and started across to Lovina.

"Is the little one lost?"

Ruby startled. She'd forgotten about the candlemaker. He had moved toward her, his expression kindly.

The girl pressed her face into Ruby's skirt. Hiding.

"Yes. I'm going to take her—" Ruby nodded to the restaurant's booth "—for a bit until her father can find her."

He didn't hesitate. "I'll go down the line and spread the word. I'm sure someone will know where her father is."

The Amish community was so tightly woven that Ruby knew it was true.

"She belongs to David Weiss. The farrier."

The man's eyes lit up. "I know him. We'll find your *daed*," he said to the girl.

Of course he knew David. Every Amish family had need of a farrier.

The girl didn't move from where her face was pressed into Ruby's skirt. Ruby laid her hand on top of the prayer *kapp* on the back of the girl's head. The covering had gone askew.

A gentle protective feeling coasted through Ruby. One similar to what she'd felt when she'd shared her lunch with Evan in the schoolyard all those years ago when he'd spilled his.

"Come along then," she said, her voice husky with the memory.

Lovina had finished with her customer and turned to Ruby as she rounded the table that separated the interior of the booth from the customers.

"Where did she come from?" Lovina asked.

Ruby shook her head. "She got separated from her *daed*. Our friend the candlemaker went to track down her father. All right if I share a cinnamon roll with her?"

"Of course." Lovina moved the one folding chair they'd brought along, and the girl climbed into it. "What's your name?"

The girl stared at her in silence.

Lovina glanced at Ruby questioningly as she unwrapped one of the cinnamon rolls.

Ruby didn't know whether it would make it worse for her to tell Lovina that the girl didn't speak. She could explain everything after this was over.

"She and her family were my customers last week." Ruby gave a cheerful smile as she put the cinnamon roll on a napkin and handed it to the girl.

"You're not Maggie, are you?"

The girl smiled shyly and shook her head.

David hadn't introduced the girls when they'd been in the restaurant, but she'd overheard him speaking to them. There had been two names beginning with the letter *M*. What was it…?

Not Margaret. Not Molly.

"Then you must be Mindy."

The girl lit up. She nodded vigorously.

Lovina stuck her hand out for Mindy to shake. "Nice to meet you."

No other customers had approached the booth, and that left Ruby free to watch as Mindy bit into the cinnamon roll. Her legs swung from the chair that was too tall for her feet to reach the ground. She'd been distracted from her tears, but how long would that last?

"Please tell me you don't have any critters in your pockets today," Ruby teased gently.

"This is the Mindy who brought a rabbit into my restaurant?" Lovina acted offended.

Mindy smiled widely. With a smudge of icing on the corner of her lip, she made a show of turning the pocket of her apron inside out.

"Whew," Ruby said with exaggerated relief.

Her gaze roamed the crowds. Surely David would be here soon. He was probably worried.

Not that taking care of Mindy was a hardship. Ruby had always enjoyed watching over her younger brother and now her niece and nephews.

She'd always thought she'd have a little girl of her own. But maybe for today, doing this good deed and showing kindness to this little one in need would be enough to fill the empty place in her heart.

David was scouring the open area between the parking lot and the large lawn where all the booths were set up when he was flagged down by Pieter King. He'd shod the young man's horse a few weeks ago, and the candlemaker wasted no time in pointing to where he'd left Mindy under the care of two young Amish women.

Mindy was safe.

Relief struck like the blast of his hammer hitting a red-hot horseshoe. His heartbeat thrummed in his ears.

He jogged through the crowds, dodging shoppers as he kept pace with Pieter. The young man seemed to understand David's urgency to reach his daughter.

David let go of every awful scenario that had swirled through his mind in a parade he never wanted to repeat. The past ten minutes had been the most terrifying of his life.

The last bit of tension he carried drained away as he caught sight of Mindy sitting on a chair inside a booth that must belong to the restaurant. One of the waitresses he recognized was waiting on an *Englisher* couple, and there was Ruby, with all her attention on Mindy, talking with animated gestures.

These were the two young Amish women who'd come to Mindy's rescue.

He thanked Pieter, then David asked the young man to track down his *daed*, who had Maggie and was also searching for Mindy.

His daughter was stuffing her mouth with a cinnamon roll that was sure to ruin her appetite for lunch. His stomach lurched when he noticed her tearstained cheeks.

Mindy saw him first since Ruby was in profile to him. Her face crumpled, and then she tossed away the rest of her cinnamon roll and scrambled underneath the table that separated him from the inside of the booth. The cloth flew up around her as she made for him.

He scooped her into his arms and crushed her to his chest. A tiny sob that escaped her, one that he felt more than heard. He rubbed his hand up and down her back. *Don't ever scare me like that again.*

He'd chide her later. Not right this moment when his emotions threatened to overwhelm him. He wasn't even sure he could speak.

Ruby rounded the table and came toward him. When he looked up, she was standing too close. Surely she would see the fire inside him, burning him up from the inside out—another example of how much a failure he was. There wasn't enough of him to go around.

Ruby's voice broke through his thoughts. "Why don't you step out from the foot traffic and catch your breath." She nodded to a wide elm tree behind the booth.

Catch his breath. Yes, that sounded *goot.* Was it even possible? And how had she guessed what he needed most?

Mindy stayed pressed against his shoulder, breath trembling as he followed Ruby to the more private place beneath that stately elm near its trunk.

He was surprised when Ruby didn't immediately return to the booth but stood not far away.

"What happened?" he asked.

"I was going to ask you that. I happened to look up and see Mindy hiding beneath the candlemaker's table across the way." Ruby nodded her head back to the thoroughfare.

"How did you know her name?" For one wild heartbeat, he thought she was going to say that

Mindy had told her. A breath later, his hope was dashed.

"I overheard you at the restaurant the other night."

That made sense. She'd been an attentive waitress, filling their glasses. She'd remembered his daughter. He could be thankful for that and for her watchful eyes this morning.

"Edvard Miller asked me to take a look at his lame horse in the parking lot, and I left the girls with my *daed*, who's here with me. He said he only turned his back for a moment, and she was gone."

His *daed* had been haggling with an *Englisher* over a hydraulic belt sander.

A sander.

It had been a long time since David had been small. Maybe he shouldn't have trusted his *daed* to watch both girls. But David hadn't wanted them underfoot while he'd been examining a horse.

David couldn't be two places at once.

He swallowed back his remorse when he realized Ruby was still talking.

"Lovina and I gave her a cinnamon roll." Her eyes were on Mindy, who was still tucked against his shoulder. "It probably ruined her appetite, but it helped distract her."

He was surprised, and Ruby must've seen it in his expression. "I have a niece and nephews."

Oh. Hadn't she said that to him at the restaurant the other night? She knew kids. Of course she would've thought of Mindy's appetite. "*Denke.* It'll be fine."

"Mindy was telling me about her new chick."

His heart pounded. For another breathless moment, hope soared. Mindy had *told* her?

Ruby must've seen the confusion and hope on his face. "She was drawing me a picture. I had some scrap paper in one of the boxes."

His hope crashed and cracked. He cleared his throat. "What a *goot* idea."

Ruby might've blushed under his praise, but it was hard to tell because she ducked her head.

His face grew hot, too. He blamed it on the sharp hope that was just now fading from his chest. He wanted Mindy to speak again. Prayed for it daily. But he didn't know how to reach her. Sometimes the hope was too painful to hold on to.

Ruby glanced up, and their eyes connected.

He felt the connection somewhere deep inside. A place that he'd shut off when Jessica had died.

It was only because of his gratefulness. Or maybe the shadow of worry for Mindy. It had been so long since he'd had someone to share his life with. All the little ups and downs. The worries and hardships.

Ruby's blush burned brighter, and he couldn't help noticing how it made the freckles across the bridge of her nose stand out. Or the soft sweep of her lashes against her cheeks when she blinked and broke the connection.

He was staring.

At that moment, his *daed* called out. David's attention was diverted as he thanked Ruby once more and went to meet his father. His stomach was tied in knots. He told himself it was only a mix of his fright and the relief at finding Mindy unharmed. But it took a long time for the knots to unravel.

Chapter Three

"*Mamm*?" David pushed through the front door.

No happy squeals from Maggie. He knew better than to hope for a tiny return shout from Mindy.

The living room was empty. He expected to find his *mamm* and the girl in the kitchen, but that was empty, too. He walked through the house and peeked inside the bedroom door that had been left ajar. He saw Mindy and Maggie lying on the floor on a pallet made with a quilt. Mindy was staring silently at her baby sister.

What was going on?

It was long past naptime, and usually his mother would've been preparing supper right now. When he pushed open the door, being careful to be quiet, he saw his mother lying in the bed. Her face had a gray pallor, and her eyes opened when she registered his movement.

"Hey. What's going on?" he asked softly.

Mindy ran to him and threw her arms around his leg. She clung to him with a ferocity that he hadn't felt in a long time, and he put one hand on top of her head, concerned.

"I felt really tired. I needed to rest. The girls were being quiet, so I asked them to lie down with me." *Mamm* pushed herself to a sitting position in the bed. Her face was still unusually pale, and David waved for her to stop even as he dislodged Mindy's arms to scoop Maggie off the floor.

"Are you coming down with something?" If his mother was ill, he didn't want to leave the girls tomorrow. Obviously, his mother needed to rest.

Mamm shook her head. "I've been getting these spells from time to time. A few hours of rest and I'm usually all right."

How long had this been happening? *Daed* had said she was tired sometimes. Not that she was having spells. What did that mean? Anger surged that he'd missed something. That *Daed* had dismissed his concerns.

"You lie back down. I'll talk to *Daed* about what we should do tomorrow."

Mindy attached herself to his leg again as he exited the bedroom. It made it difficult to walk, having her glued to his leg, and he only made it halfway down the hall before he had to gently disentangle her. Late afternoon sunlight slanted through the open living room windows, and he saw the dried tear tracks on Mindy's cheeks.

His heart constricted.

He squatted, still with Maggie in one arm. He knew if he put her down, she would just scream until he picked her up.

"It's okay. *Daed's* here now. *Grossmammi* says she just needs to rest."

Mindy clung to his shoulder with her little hands. She was trembling a little, and he slipped his arm around her waist to hug her.

"Were you scared?"

He wished she would answer him, though he knew she wouldn't. He held her close for as long as he could, hoping his presence was enough to reassure her. He felt inadequate. Jessica would've known what to say, what to do to reassure their daughter.

He needed to talk to *Daed*. But Maggie started kicking up a fuss when they went through the kitchen, and David realized the girls hadn't eaten, though he'd been a little late from his last appointment of the day.

He stopped in the barn anyway, with Mindy clinging to his leg and Maggie fussing from his arms.

"*Mamm* can't keep the girls if she's sick," he

said quietly while *Daed* measured and marked a board.

"She isn't sick."

Was *Daed* in denial? *Mamm* was not herself. Maybe *Daed* just didn't want to see it.

"I could hire someone. A nanny."

"No." *Daed's* answer was strident. He kept working. "Your *mamm* loves being with the girls. And family takes care of family."

His *daed* seemed to think that was the end of it, because he flipped on a pneumatic saw. David was left with two hungry, upset girls and no solutions.

Why had he even tried?

He needed to get the girls fed, and he wanted to erase the terrified expression from Mindy's face and from his memory. Maybe that's why he ended up sitting in Ruby's section in the restaurant.

The restaurant was bustling, and the hostess who sat them at their table ended up bringing their drinks and some sweet rolls for the girls to munch on.

Several minutes and eating the rolls seemed to have put some color back in Mindy's face. She looked around the restaurant, watching other patrons. Or was she looking for something? She was craning her neck to see all around.

He needed a moment to gather himself and

was grateful for her distraction. Weariness overtook him, and he wiped one hand down his face.
He could stay home with the girls tomorrow. It
wasn't ideal, but if it gave *Mamm* time to rest,
maybe it was what he needed to do.

Lost in his thoughts, he didn't hear Ruby ap-
proach from behind him, didn't realize she was
there until Mindy stood up on her chair. As the
waitress passed by David's elbow, the little girl
launched out of her seat toward Ruby. David
made an unintelligible noise, reaching out one
ineffective hand.

Ruby reacted quickly and swept his daughter
up in her arms with a surprised "Umph!"

Relief flared and he started to get up from the
table, ready to reprimand Mindy. She shouldn't
have jumped like that. What if Ruby hadn't
caught her? She could have been injured.

Ruby had the beginnings of a smile on her
lips, but then her expression changed to one of
concern. He realized at the same moment that
Mindy was crying, her soft sobs muffled against
Ruby's shoulder. Her arms clung to the young
woman's neck.

Ruby tilted her head back toward his seat
as if she wanted him to sit. He settled back as
she slipped into the seat across from him, with
Mindy tucked in her arms. Her order pad was

pressed against the girl's back, and she used the other hand to smooth Mindy's hair.

David's face was burning as he registered stares from two of the nearby tables.

Ruby mouthed, *What's going on?*

He was baffled by Mindy's behavior, shocked that she would cling to someone she barely knew. He'd thought she had calmed down. But this outburst of emotion had come from somewhere.

"I think she had a scare today." Everything inside him was tight and twisted up that his own daughter couldn't tell him what was wrong. "When I arrived to pick up the girls, my *mamm* was lying down. She said she got tired, and the girls were in the room with her. They seemed okay…" His words trailed off. Obviously, Mindy wasn't okay.

Mindy's soft sobs had begun to quiet under Ruby's gentle ministrations. Being held and her head being rubbed.

Family takes care of family.

The thought hit uncomfortably in David's chest. Why had it popped into his head now, watching Ruby with his daughter?

"I'm sorry about this." The words burned his throat. "We don't mean to take you away from your customers."

Ruby's eyes darted to two corners of the restaurant before her gaze settled back on him. "The customers can wait for a few minutes. Most of them have families. They'll understand."

It was kind of her to say so. She shouldn't have to comfort his daughter. The place behind David's nose burned at the realization that his daughter wanted Ruby and not him.

Maggie plopped in his lap, pieces of sweet roll in her fists. She babbled, her words incomprehensible but happy now that her sister seemed settled.

"You're really good with her."

Ruby rested her cheek on top of Mindy's head for a moment. "My niece and I are very close."

"You like kids." It was obvious from her gentle way with his daughter and the patience she'd shown the other day at the farmers market.

There was some shadow in Ruby's eyes as she nodded slightly.

Ruby looked at the man in front of her. Really looked at him for the first time without the distraction of his daughter or worries about the other patrons.

David looked weary. As if he had the weight of the world on his shoulders. There were lines around his mouth and eyes. It was clear how much he loved his daughters and was worried about Mindy. Ruby's heart squeezed for the little girl in her arms.

Mindy's sobs quieted to an occasional sniffle, her body now limp. Ruby had already been warm from running back and forth to take care of her tables. Now she started to sweat and felt her dress cling to her in every place that Mindy pressed against her.

"Is she—she's falling asleep." David's voice was disbelieving.

Lovina was waiting tables on the other side of the restaurant. Ruby saw her scanning the room and caught the moment when her eyes lit on her. Something passed over her expression, but she smiled at the table closest to her—one of Ruby's tables—and moved to fill their water cups.

Ruby didn't want her friend or other coworkers to have to pick up her slack, but it was also more than obvious that Mindy had needed comfort from Ruby. She just didn't know why.

"Leave her be," Ruby said quietly. "She must need to rest. I can put in your order to go, and you can take the girls home in a bit."

He nodded, serious. "That's probably a *goot* idea."

Maggie seemed distracted with playing with her sweet roll.

David glanced down, suddenly vulnerable. "You probably think I'm a horrible father. Losing track of Mindy at the farmers market and now this."

"Of course I don't. You've got a lot on your plate."

He rubbed one finger on the tabletop, speaking as if the words were difficult for him to say. "She was there when her mother passed."

Ruby's gaze darted to Maggie, who was paying them no attention, and Mindy had gone completely limp against Ruby.

"I'm sorry. I don't know why I said that," David said, seeming rattled. He blew out a gusty sigh. "I don't know how to reach her. She won't talk to me. Clearly, she's taken with you." He rubbed one hand down over his mouth.

"It's like what happened today brought everything back for her," he mumbled to himself.

"If you need someone to watch the girls—" *I'll do it.*

Emma scurried past the table. "You've got two orders up."

David glanced around as if he'd forgotten where they were. He seemed to shake himself.

"If you would just put in an order of chicken-fried steak and a grilled cheese for the girls," he said, his voice apologetic.

He was clearly finished with this conversation, looking embarrassed. He slid out of his side of the booth and reached for Mindy.

His hands brushed against Ruby's when she transferred the girl into his arms. Mindy stirred but didn't wake up. Ruby rushed off to the kitchen to put in their order and serve her other tables.

What had she been thinking, offering to help with the girls? They weren't her business, even if Mindy made a beeline toward Ruby every time she saw her.

But as the night wore on, she couldn't stop thinking about Mindy's sobs or the way the girl had felt cuddled up in her arms.

Why was she feeling so muddled? Her emotions were close to the surface today because *Daed* had begun moving furniture around. That had to be it. He'd carted a rocking chair from the *daadi haus* into the big house and moved two chests from his room out into the smaller home. He'd asked Ruby whether she would pack up some of her books and things to move, but she'd put him off.

Ruby had found herself lingering over the linen closet, fingering one of *Mamm's* quilts folded on the shelf. It was like leaving *Mamm* behind. Or maybe leaving Ruby's childhood hopes and dreams behind.

It hurt.

She hadn't spoken to him about Lovina's idea of them moving into an apartment together. There was a part of her that wanted to do it, but something held her back.

After the dinner rush had died down, Ruby was

between customers and was rolling silverware on an empty table in the back of the restaurant. Lovina came to help her, at first simply sidling next to Ruby and working on the silverware.

"You okay?"

Ruby nodded. "Thanks for covering for me earlier."

Silent for a moment, Lovina finally said, "That girl certainly likes you."

Ruby kept her gaze on the fork and knife under her fingertips. "She was upset tonight."

"And only you could comfort her?" There was something in Lovina's words. A faint accusation, maybe.

Ruby was surprised by it. "I'm sorry if I held up a couple of tables." She didn't regret giving Mindy comfort. The little girl had been through so much, losing her mother so young.

Lovina was quiet for a long time. For the first time, there was tension between the two women.

"I saw the way you looked at him."

Ruby shook her head, perplexed. "Who?"

"The farrier."

"How was I looking at him?" She'd listened to him, tried to show compassion in the scant few minutes she'd been at his table.

Lovina shrugged.

What was going on with her tonight? Ruby felt confused by this entire conversation.

"Maybe we should wait to think about getting an apartment," Lovina said suddenly. "You could still change your mind and marry someone. Like the farrier."

"I don't want to marry David Weiss." The words were out before she'd even thought them.

"My cousin married a widower." Lovina did not even pretend to work with the silverware. Her hands were flat on the table, and she stared at Ruby.

"She had an old friend from her school days who had lost his wife. She really wanted a family. And she got one, by marrying him."

Ruby shook her head. "You know I'm never going to marry anyone. My perfect match is— gone."

Lovina had a stubborn set to her jaw. "You've said before how you always wanted a family. Maybe that little girl is your chance to have it. Not everyone gets a love match."

But when Lovina said the words, there was an edge to them.

And the words hurt. Lovina knew about Ruby's loss. "It isn't like that between David and me." They were barely acquaintances. "And I was only trying to help with Mindy tonight."

Maybe Ruby's words were sharper than she intended, because Lovina flinched.

Ruby immediately felt remorse. She bowed her head. "I'm sorry."

"So am I," Lovina said stiffly.

Lovina finished the last two sets of silverware in silence, and Ruby felt awful about the rift between them.

Maybe that little girl is your chance to have a family.

Lovina's words cut more than they should. Ruby told herself it was only because of everything that had happened earlier in the day. Ruby's grief was fresh and painful.

She did still want a family. That desire had never left, even after Jonathan's death.

Her perfect match was gone. And that was that.

Wasn't it?

Chapter Four

Maybe that little girl is your chance to have a family.

Ruby couldn't get Lovina's ridiculous comment out of her head, and it had been several days. Several days where she and Lovina exchanged polite small talk at the restaurant.

There was still a weird tension between them. Ruby hadn't realized Lovina had wanted to share an apartment that badly. They'd only begun talking about it. Or was it something deeper? Was Lovina resentful of Ruby's hypothetical chance to have a family?

It wasn't going to happen.

And Ruby couldn't put her *daed* off any longer. She'd toted entire shelves of books out to the *daadi haus* yesterday during her hours off from the restaurant.

It was Sunday morning, and she'd had to refocus her mind, too many times to count, on the sermon delivered by Brother Glick, one of the grandfatherly men from the community. Finally, he seemed to be nearing the end of it.

Hannah shifted restlessly in the folding chair next to Ruby. The Grantham family was hosting this week's service, and their basement was on the small side. Ruby was elbow to elbow with her niece on one side and Beth on the other.

And it was stuffy. Ruby hadn't drawn a breath of fresh air since she'd traipsed down the basement stairs. That had to be why her mind was so easily distracted.

That and the fact that David and his daughters had slipped inside as the service was beginning. Mindy and Maggie were tucked close to their father on the men's side of the room, their skirts and *kapps* out of place among the dark trousers, homespun shirts and bearded faces.

Maggie dozed, sitting on her father's thigh with her head lolled against the inside of his arm. Mindy sat with her hands clasped on her lap, her feet swinging slowly above the floor. Her gaze wandered around the room as light as a butterfly in flight.

She didn't smile.

Ruby hadn't really noticed the girl, not in more than a passing way, before their encounter at the farmers market. Mindy had smiled that morning, but Ruby hadn't seen a hint of a smile since.

Maybe that little girl is your chance to have a family.

It was as if Lovina, sitting one row behind her and several seats down, had pricked Ruby with her gaze.

That was a fanciful thought. Lovina was probably paying better attention to the sermon than Ruby was.

Why wouldn't her outlandish statement leave Ruby alone?

Mindy was clearly lonely and had a deep sadness in her heart. David had said she'd been present when her mother had passed. That must've been terrifying.

It was clear from how she'd behaved with Ruby that she craved a woman's touch. A mother's touch.

But that woman wasn't Ruby.

Was it?

Ruby must've shifted in her chair, because Lily glanced sharply at her over Hannah's head.

What was she even thinking? David must still be mired in grief for his late wife. He'd made no indication that he thought of Ruby as more than a passing acquaintance. He was thankful for her help, and that was it.

If…*if* Ruby was actually considering Lovina's

wild idea, what was she supposed to do? Walk up to the man and propose they get married for Mindy's sake?

He might laugh in her face. Or be offended that she'd seen he was struggling on his own.

Her palms felt sweaty even considering it.

No.

No, she wasn't going to do it.

She wasn't even going to think it anymore.

"We'll dismiss for today's picnic." Brother Glick must've finished his sermon, and she hadn't noticed.

Hannah sat up straighter, and there was a small buzz of whispers and movement from the other children all around.

The Granthams had planned for all the families to stay and eat a picnic together. The pleasant autumn weather had held, and Ruby was looking forward to visiting with friends and being with her brother Reuben and his wife Theresa and their children.

Hannah ran up to Ruby and hugged her. "I brought another picture for you to look at."

"I can't wait," Ruby said.

As everyone moved up the stairs and out into the sunshine, Ruby was aware of David among the crowd in front of her. She could see his head and shoulders above the people between them.

He held Maggie in one arm. When he smiled down on Mindy, Ruby felt a twist in her gut.

She blamed Lovina's suggestion for her extra awareness of him.

Women spread picnic blankets across the yard, and daughters helped unload baskets of food from family buggies. Men stood in groups talking as young boys and girls darted through, playing tag and stretching their legs after a long spell sitting in worship.

Ruby had her arms full with the overloaded picnic basket and had almost made it to the quilt where Lily was setting out plates and silverware when a child-sized projectile hit her legs from the side.

Mindy wrapped her arms around Ruby's legs and she wobbled on her feet. She was off-kilter, and the heavy picnic basket was going to topple her.

Except a strong pair of hands clasped her wrists and steadied her. She found herself blinking up into David's blue eyes.

"Mindy, you can't run into people like that," he chided her.

"Here," Lily said, quickly rising to take the basket from Ruby as David tried to untangle his daughter from her skirts.

"It's all right," Ruby said.

As the girl finally backed away, she realized

Mindy was sniffling, and there were tears on her cheeks.

"I didn't realize we'd sat so close." David motioned to the picnic blanket right next to Lily and Ruby's blanket. "We'd better move, or she'll be bugging you the entire meal."

"You don't need to do that." Ruby was aware of Lily's sharp, curious gaze on the back of her head. Beth was nearby, too, settling a blanket for herself and Evan and *Daed*. But it was Mindy's tearstained face that tugged at Ruby's heartstrings.

Mindy grabbed Ruby's hand and tugged, pointing to the edge of her father's picnic blanket.

"No, no," David said quickly.

"Hi there. Do you want to play with my Jacob?" Lily pointed to her son who was playing Duck Duck Goose with two other small children nearby.

Mindy shook her head and kept tugging on Ruby's hand.

David frowned, his gaze clearly apologetic. "I'm sorry," he muttered. He reached for Mindy, but Ruby stayed him with a touch on the back of his hand.

His gaze flew to hers, and she jerked her hand away.

Her blush burned hotter.

"What about this?" She crouched to speak to Mindy face-to-face.

Mindy sniffled and watched Ruby's face.

"You pull your picnic blanket closer, and we can all eat together. How about that?" She directed the question to David.

Maybe it was too forward, but it was the easiest solution she could think of.

David seemed relieved that Mindy's tears were being blinked away.

"If you're sure."

Ruby caught a speaking glance from Lily and realized she'd just put herself in an awkward position. Even Beth was watching with veiled curiosity from her blanket. She hadn't told her family about what had happened at the farmers market or at the restaurant. She'd wanted to keep those sweet moments with Mindy for herself.

But they were clearly going to find out now because of Mindy's familiarity.

And they would have so many questions later. What had she gotten herself into?

Quick introductions were made. David met Ruby's brothers Evan and Aaron and sister-in-laws Lily and Beth. David shook Noah Kauffman's hand as everyone settled on the blankets to eat.

David saw the discomfort in Ruby's expression

and thought about simply packing up the girls and leaving the picnic. But Mindy was curled up next to Ruby's thigh, and he didn't have the heart to pull her away. Not yet.

She'd been subdued all morning, ever since they'd stopped by *Daed* and *Mamm's* to see if they wanted to ride to worship together and found *Mamm* still in bed. *Daed* insisted she just needed a day to rest.

David wasn't so sure. He'd urged his father to take her to see Dr. Bradshaw, the local family practitioner. *Daed* had only shook his head. Uncommunicative as always.

David had spent the drive to church fuming and the sermon repenting. Why did things always have to be so difficult between him and *Daed*?

Now set on her own two feet, Maggie shuffled across the blanket to Ruby, who lifted the girl onto her lap, not pushing Mindy out of her place.

David was left to sort out the food. After a morning of rushing the girls through getting dressed and trying to clean up after breakfast and then keeping them quiet and still during worship, he was grateful for the short break.

He passed a peanut-butter-and-jelly sandwich to Ruby, and she promptly tore it in half and gave one piece to each girl. Mindy chomped on hers happily while Maggie tore her sandwich apart, exposing the gooey insides. Had he put napkins in the basket?

"I didn't realize you two were friends," Beth said. It sounded as if she were fishing for information.

"We aren't," Ruby said quickly. She must've caught his scrunched brows, because she quickly said, "David and the girls have been in my section at the restaurant several times. The girls are precious, but David and I are still getting to know each other."

David smiled when the sister-in-law's gaze flitted to him, laced with some skepticism. What was that about?

"My girls have had a hard time since their *mamm* passed. Mindy is especially drawn to Ruby, and your sister-in-law is kind enough to spend a few extra minutes with her when she is able."

Ruby seemed to be trying to tell Lily something with only her eyes as she handed her a plate piled high with fried chicken and a salad, plus mashed potatoes. Ruby held the plate above Mindy's head and raised her elbow just before Maggie would've bumped into her. She must've seen his longing look toward the chicken—one of his favorite foods—because she passed the plate on to him.

He tried to stop her with a raised hand, but she

pushed the plate toward him with some urgency, and he had no choice but to take it. "I can't."

"There's plenty to go around," said Ruby.

"I've got some fresh watermelon in here." He pointed to the basket. He was a little embarrassed that he hadn't planned better for this picnic. He'd forgotten about it until just before they were going to leave and thrown in what he could find. Peanut-butter-and-jelly sandwiches, the watermelon he'd sliced yesterday at lunchtime and some leftover corn on the cob from their meal last night.

Lily sure seemed interested in their interaction. She was watching them closely. "Ruby is wonderful with children, isn't she? I keep telling her that she doesn't need to work at the restaurant. We would love for her to be home with us all the time."

Something passed between the two women—he didn't know what—and Ruby looked down at her lap while she chewed her next bite.

Mindy pointed at the mashed potatoes on Ruby's plate, and Ruby passed her a spoon and turned her plate toward the girl, who eagerly reached for them. Mindy sometimes ate with gusto and sometimes ate very little, and he never knew what kind of a day it was going to be. Apparently, she was hungry today.

"Here, Mindy girl. Why don't you eat *Daed's* potatoes?" he urged.

Mindy shook her head with a stubborn tilt of her chin.

"It's all right," Ruby said quietly.

She used the corner of her apron to wipe jelly from Maggie's hands when the girl gesticulated wildly. Ruby laughed and tweaked the girl's nose.

Ruby had a way with Maggie. She was a natural caregiver. But again, he felt a bit of apprehension. He probably shouldn't let Mindy have so much time with Ruby, not when nothing could come of it. He didn't want Mindy to fall back into a place of sadness when Ruby didn't have time for them because of her work at the restaurant. Or when she began starting a family of her own.

He found himself scrutinizing the young woman. She had to be twenty at least. A little older than he and Jessica had been when they had married. Not all Amish girls married when they were seventeen or eighteen, but many did. Did Ruby have a beau? He hadn't given that any thought, but something about it made his insides twist.

The long sweep of her lashes against her cheek and the strands of dark hair that had escaped from beneath her *kapp* and curled around her face drew his gaze. She was beautiful. He had been so wrapped up in the girls that he hadn't noticed it before, but it shone bright in her gentle spirit, and suddenly he was uncomfortable enough that he had to shift on the picnic blanket. He hadn't noticed anyone since Jessica. He didn't know what to do with the uncomfortable feeling swirling through him, the awareness of her femininity and delicate features.

What was he even thinking?

He'd tried not to become like his father—closed off and silent. But after Jessica's death, David had retreated inside himself. He couldn't open his heart again to someone only to have it shattered later. He couldn't do it to himself or to the girls.

"I was hoping to see your *daed* here today," Noah said from the next blanket over. "I need to see about having a small nightstand built for my bedroom."

A shadow passed over Ruby's expression, quickly gone as she focused on Maggie now playing patty-cake.

"My *mamm* wasn't feeling well," David explained. "*Daed* stayed home with her."

Mindy tipped her head up at him, eyes squinted. He had tried to reassure her this morning, knowing she'd been emotional after *Mamm's* tired spell almost a week ago.

"I don't know if *Mamm* will be up to keeping you tomorrow," he said to Mindy.

Ruby was watching with compassion. "If you need help with the girls, I would be happy to watch them. I am off from the restaurant tomorrow."

Lily leaned toward them. He had almost forgotten about her presence and wondered how much she had seen over the last few minutes.

She smiled, but there was something calculating behind the expression. "Of course you could bring the girls over tomorrow. Ruby could watch them at my house. Seth and Hannah would love to have them visit. We have a lot of toys, and they'd be welcome for as long as you need."

Ruby looked as if she meant to say something but stifled it and looked down. Her smile was muted somehow.

Mindy had overheard and was nodding vigorously. She pressed her hand under her chin and turned pleading eyes on David.

He felt a little pressured, but he didn't have anyone to watch the girls tomorrow, and *Mamm* had frightened him this morning with how pale she'd been.

Mindy wanted to go. He should set aside his own discomfort with the idea for her benefit.

And hope it wasn't a mistake.

Chapter Five

David was late, and every clop of his horse's hooves on the country road only served to remind him of a ticking second hand on a clock.

Ten days had passed since the Sunday afternoon picnic and Ruby's kind offer to watch the girls. She'd kept them several times during the past week and a half.

Because *Mamm* was ill.

Helpless and angry, he'd used precious minutes to stop by and check on *Mamm* after a long day shoeing horses.

She had been sitting up at the kitchen table, drinking a cup of tea. She had news. The doctor had been by, and the man had some concerns about her heart and wanted her to rest more.

David brought up hiring a nanny. He'd mentioned it to *Daed*, but not to *Mamm*. Until now. She'd refused the offer and insisted that watching the girls wasn't too much for her. How could David believe her?

He knew how much she loved them, knew she wanted to help him. *Family takes care of family.* *Daed's* words were always with him.

But the girls were his responsibility.

He'd gone out to the workshop, where his father had been rubbing stain into a wooden chest of drawers. *Daed* had been quiet, as usual. Was he grief-stricken? A heart condition wasn't a small thing. Angry?

How could David ever know?

"Do you think *Mamm* should see a specialist?" He'd asked the question because Dr. Bradshaw was getting close to retirement. He was old-fashioned, which was why many of the Amish folk liked him. He made house calls and didn't argue when they wanted to use home remedies that were tried and tested.

But for something as serious as a heart condition, wouldn't *Mamm* and *Daed* want a second opinion?

Daed had shook his head and kept staining.

David had barely kept the reins on his temper. "You can't let her give up. I still need *Mamm.* The girls do, too."

But his demand had gotten no response from his father. David had clenched his fists against the awful energy coursing through him.

Maybe his father had sensed the depths of his frustration, because he'd said, "Your *mamm* wants to try the medicine Doc Bradshaw gave her. And rest."

And that was all his father had to say. No words of comfort. That *Mamm* would be all right.

Watching the girls was never restful. Mindy was a busy little girl who loved to be in the kitchen and help cook, explore outside, run around, swing, the list went on. Maggie was a handful, too. She wanted to run after Mindy and join in whatever she was doing.

Maybe he should hire a nanny anyway. Would it matter if he made his parents angry if it kept *Mamm* from pushing herself too hard?

After fifteen minutes in the buggy, he still didn't have any answers. And it was too late to find any, because he turned the buggy into Ruby's drive.

He set the brake and made sure the horse was settled, then followed the sound of voices around the side of the house.

Not voices. Giggling. That sounded like… He drew up short when he found Ruby and Mindy, along with a little girl who belonged to Lily and Aaron on a quilt spread in the shade of the house.

Ruby caught sight of him first, as Mindy and the other little girl were too busy. In between them on the blanket was what appeared to be a gray barnyard cat in a doll's dress with a bonnet tied around its head.

The scowling face of the cat wasn't what was amazing. It was Mindy's giggles. That sound coming from a girl who'd been silent and grieving for so long was something he'd longed to hear, and he couldn't help the tears burning the backs of his eyes.

Ruby recognized it. He saw it in her eyes before she looked down at her charges. "Girls, it's time to let Mr. Whiskers go back to the barn."

She reached for the cat and got a scratch on the back of her hand for her troubles.

Mindy and the other little girl seemed content to watch Ruby quickly pull the bonnet off the cat and then wrestle it free of the dress.

David squatted next to the picnic blanket, and Mindy leaned into his chest for a hug.

Everything he'd been thinking in the buggy, all those worries, flitted away at the sound of Mindy's giggles and the feel of this hug.

All because of Ruby.

She must've felt his stare, because she blushed sweetly and looked away, idly folding the little doll's dress between her hands.

"I'm guessing that wasn't your idea." He quirked his brows.

She laughed a little. "Good guess. The girls decided to dress up the kitty, and I didn't want either of them to get scratched up. He played nice for longer than I thought he would."

"But you were the one that got scratched." David tapped his index finger on the back of her hand. Awareness zipped up his arm, and the baby hairs at the back of his neck stood up.

He'd felt the same awareness at the picnic last Sunday and was just as unprepared for it today as he had been then.

Ruby seemed to feel it, too. Her eyes darted to his face before she glanced away.

"*Aendi* Ruby likes cats," said the little girl whose name he couldn't remember.

He cleared his throat and wished he could clear his mind of this awareness of her as easily. "Just not rabbits?" he teased gently.

Ruby pulled a face. "Not in a restaurant."

Had that really been weeks ago?

Mindy tugged at David's shirt sleeve, commanding without words. He glanced down to see the paper she pushed into his hands. He realized that the picnic blanket was also littered with paper, carefully weighted down by a basket of wooden blocks. Crayons were strewn across the ground. He looked at the picture. He recognized Mindy's artwork. She had drawn three crude stick figures.

"That's you," Ruby tapped the tallest of the figures. "And Mindy and Maggie."

Mindy was watching his face carefully, waiting for his reaction.

He smiled at her. "It's wonderful. I'll find a tack and hang it in the living room when we get home."

Mindy beamed.

"Oh, you're here." Lily walked around the side of the house.

"I'm sorry I'm late," David said.

She looked between him and Ruby.

"I was giving Maggie and Seth a snack, and she was nodding off in the high chair. I hope it won't mess up her bedtime, but I put her down for a nap about a half hour ago."

"That's fine."

"Hannah you're all dirty," Lily said. "Why don't you come in and wash up? You, too, Mindy. You can help me wake up your sister. I'm sure your *daed* wants to get home."

This was said with a pointed look between him and Ruby.

He didn't know how to interpret it.

And then Mindy happily bounced behind Lily and Hannah, leaving him alone with Ruby.

She bent to gather up papers. He knelt to pick crayons out of the grass beside the blanket.

"You've been good for her," he observed. "For Mindy."

"She's a darling. But why does she like to dress up animals?"

Her question startled a rusty laugh out of him. "I don't know. I think she read about it in a book once."

Ruby had made him laugh. And Mindy.

"I haven't heard her giggling since..." That hot feeling was back in his throat, and he couldn't finish. He cleared his throat. "Thank you. I hope she didn't run you too ragged."

"She does love animals, doesn't she? We visited the barn twice to count the horses and see the milk cow."

He could easily imagine that.

For a moment, observing Mindy's joy and Ruby's easy way with her, he'd forgotten about *Mamm* and his need for childcare during the days.

But...

Ruby was good with the girls.

His *mamm* needed at least a few weeks of rest.

Ruby had been kind enough to watch the girls during her spare time. What if he could make it worth her while to take some time off from the restaurant? Perhaps she'd agree to be a short-term nanny.

"I know you enjoy working at the restaurant," he started hesitantly. "But... I wonder if we could make some kind of deal while my *mamm* is recovering."

Ruby seemed to square her shoulders. "Actually, I wanted to talk to you about that."

Ruby was aware that Lily could come back outside at any time. She probably only had a few moments alone with David before they were besieged with young children again.

Maybe that little girl is your chance to have a family.

Things had still been strained between Ruby and Lovina at the restaurant. The closeness they'd shared was missing. One night last week, Ruby had witnessed Emma and Naomi flirting with a table of young Amish men, and she'd turned to make a teasing comment about it to Lovina only to remember that Lovina probably wouldn't want her to.

It wasn't that they weren't speaking. But they weren't speaking.

Daed was still slowly moving his things out into the *daadi haus*. And Ruby couldn't stop thinking of Lovina's words.

Maybe that little girl is your chance to have a family.

Ruby had thought she could be content as things were. Growing old single alongside *Daed*.

Until Mindy and Maggie had gotten past the walls of her heart and settled in.

She straightened and tried not to focus on

how close they were on the picnic blanket as she quickly slipped a piece of construction paper that had been folded into fourths from her apron pocket. She smoothed it out flat and held it out for David to take.

He looked down at the paper in his big calloused hands. She already knew what was on it.

"Mindy drew it."

"I know." His voice sounded hoarse.

There were four stick figures on that page, unlike the one Mindy had shown him earlier.

"I asked her who each of the people in the picture were. Well, I guessed, and she let me know if I got it right or wrong."

His head tipped toward her slightly, and she took that as a sign to go on, especially when he tapped the first figure.

"That's Mindy," Ruby said. The stick figures stood all in a row, their hands touching.

David tapped the next tallest figure.

"That's you."

He skipped to the fourth figure, the one on the far right.

"That's Maggie."

He hesitated minutely, and she was standing close enough to hear the catch in his breath just before he tapped the last figure. The one between the drawings of David and Maggie.

"That's me," she whispered. "I thought it might be her mother."

A muscle in his jaw ticked. He dropped the paper to his side and she rushed on, "Then I asked if it was her grandmother. Or a friend. And she pointed to me."

Ruby had stared at the drawing for a beat too long. She'd looked into Mindy's dear face and then hugged the girl around the shoulders.

"We could get married," she blurted.

Her cheeks burned as he stared at her, not open-mouthed with shock but close. He was flushed, too.

A happy shriek from the other side of the wall startled them both.

"Walk to my buggy with me," he murmured.

She barely heard it over the pounding of her heart in her ears. Had she really said that? What must he think of her?

She fell into step beside him. He'd brought Mindy and Maggie on three days this week, but she'd never had the opportunity to simply walk beside him. He was so *tall*, his shoulders and arms muscled from the work he did.

Their steps were muffled by the dry fall grasses. Silence stretched.

And stretched.

It quickly grew uncomfortable.

"I've grown fond of the girls," she said when

he still didn't say anything. "I don't think Mindy would be opposed to the idea, not after she drew that picture."

He looked down and seemed surprised to realize he still held the picture.

"I was thinking of hiring a nanny," he said. "If you quit your job at the restaurant, I could pay you—"

She was aware of the skin of her face, stretched too tight over her bones. "That would mean trading one job for another. And…and then I'd have to find another family to care for if you married someone else one day."

He shook his head, his eyes unhappy. "I don't want to marry again. I don't want to get married at all."

Oh.

She blinked rapidly and averted her face. She must be tomato red by now with how hot she was blushing.

"I don't—" He exhaled noisily. "You surprised me. I'm not saying no."

He isn't?

They had almost reached his buggy, and she drew to a stop before they got too close to the massive horse hitched to it.

"Family takes care of family," he muttered so softly she barely caught the words.

"What?"

He shook his head and looked down at Mindy's drawing again. "My *mamm* is sick. She has a heart condition."

Oh, David. He said the words with almost no inflection, but she knew he must be hurting.

"If we married—what am I even saying?" He tipped his head back so he was looking up at the sky. "This is *lecherich*. I don't want to get married again."

She wished for the ground to open up and swallow her whole.

He suddenly turned a sharp gaze on her. "What about you? You're young and pretty. I understand that what you're proposing would be for the girls, but what if there was someone else who came along. Your true love?"

She folded her hands in front of her and looked at him straight on. "There won't be anybody like that for me. I've already resigned myself to it. This will be a convenient marriage for both of us."

He seemed taken aback. "Why isn't there someone for you?"

Her lips trembled a bit, but she pressed them together. "My perfect match was Jonathan Miller. He died almost ten years ago."

An echo of her grief passed over his expression. "I'm sorry."

"I'm sorry, too. For you." The sharpness of what she'd lost had faded, but his grief must still be fresh. "That's why I thought this idea might work. For Mindy. And Maggie."

He lifted the drawing that had been at his side. Stared at the picture again.

"I lost my chance to have a perfect match. And you and the girls lost their mother."

There was the grief pulsing behind his eyes. Anger, too. And something else.

Giggles and happy shrieks exploded as Mindy and Hannah tumbled out the front door. Lily emerged to stand on the front porch holding a sleepy Maggie on her hip. Her expression was stormy as she looked to where Ruby and David stood. Lily had asked dozens of questions over the past week, all about Ruby's connection with David. She still wanted Ruby to be a live-in nanny for her and Aaron.

Mindy caught sight of her father, and her face lit up with joy.

Some tension inside the man standing beside Ruby ratcheted higher.

"You're good for her," he murmured as they both watched Mindy race toward them.

Ruby had made her outlandish proposal. He hadn't said no, but he hadn't said yes, either.

"What if we did a trial period?" she asked.

"Such as?"

"Three dates. Spend time together to see whether we'd even get along—as a family." Her words faltered as the enormity of what she'd suggested settled over her.

Marrying David would mean forever. A lifetime of living in the same house with a man she barely knew. What she did know of him was good. He loved his daughters deeply. He was well respected in the community.

But was he grumpy in the mornings? Did he expect his house to be kept perfectly? Would he treat her with the same kindness he showed the girls?

Mindy threw herself at David, and he swept her up in his arms and swung her around before settling her on his hip.

Ruby's heart bumped.

David met her gaze once more. "Three dates."

She nodded, a sudden lump in her throat. *He agrees?* "I'll see you on Sunday, then? Goodbye, Mindy."

She met Lily in the yard and toted Maggie to her father, who had already settled Mindy in the buggy. Awareness tickled her senses as the warmth of David's hand brushed against her bare arm when he took the babe from her. Aware of the way his glance landed on her now that they had this…what? Secret? Arrangement? Whatever it was, it was between them and no one else.

She waved as the trio drove away, knowing that everything was about to change.

Chapter Six

David helped Ruby into the buggy in the Kauffman's driveway, her hand cool to the touch as he guided her up.

Their eyes met for a moment before her gaze skittered away.

It had been eight years since he had courted Jessica. He had forgotten how to do this.

He planned to take Ruby to the restaurant where she worked and only today had realized that it might be awkward for her to be there with him and the girls while her coworkers waited on her. He was also certain he wasn't supposed to have brought his daughters on a date, but with his *mamm* still not at her regular energy level, he had been too embarrassed to ask one of the other young ladies from church. He hadn't wanted to endure the questions if they asked him what he was doing.

Not when he didn't even know himself.

After Jessica, he'd promised himself that he would never open his heart again. But what Ruby had suggested—after he'd gotten over the initial shock of it—made sense. They would both go into these dates with no intention of falling in love. Theirs would be a platonic marriage. One that benefited both of them.

"Hello there," Ruby greeted his daughters cheerfully. He had warned her on the doorstep that they were waiting in the buggy.

She sounded completely happy to see the girls. Wouldn't he have heard it in her voice if she was frustrated at their presence?

Maybe he had been a little selfish in bringing them along. He was nervous.

This wasn't a real courtship. But that didn't stop his heart from pounding or his palms from sweating. He thought having the girls along might make things easier.

Mindy was leaning into Ruby's side, and Maggie gurgled happily from the car seat he'd strapped to the backseat bench. Not all Amish used car seats in their buggies, but he'd quickly realized that he'd needed more hands than he had after Jessica died. Maggie was safer in the seat.

He flipped the reins, and the horse set out at a trot.

"Did you have a *goot* day today?" Ruby directed the question toward Mindy, who nodded enthusiastically. She pressed a drawing into Ruby's hands.

"Oh, look at all your animals! And there's your bunny in a dress." Ruby shared a conspiratorial smile with him over Mindy's head.

He and Mindy and Maggie had spent the morning at his parents' house, and David had realized all over again just how bad the shape everything was in. That familiar heaviness settled on him now. He'd stopped wishing a long time ago for a brother to share the burden. Tonight it just felt heavy.

"And what about you?"

It took David a moment to realize she was directing her question toward him.

"How was your day?"

He kept his eyes on the road as emotion swamped him. "Fine." He cleared his throat. Surely he could do better than that. "I saw Elijah Glick's mare late this afternoon. She's due to foal in a few weeks. I'll help him with that."

"I thought you only shoed horses."

He shrugged under her curious gaze. "Started out that way, but folks always have questions about other ailments for their horses—and other animals sometimes, too. I read a lot of veterinary books when I can get my hands on them."

"Hmm." Was that an impressed *hmm* or a disgruntled one? He didn't know.

Mindy tugged on Ruby's sleeve to get her attention. Ruby told a story about her nephew deciding to give one of the baby hogs a bath in his *mamm's* washtub. She pulled both him and Mindy into her story, and he found himself smiling.

A few minutes later, Maggie's cheerful burbles had turned into a pitiful "yah, yah, yah" that seemed to grow louder every second.

"I'm sorry," he muttered. "I forgot to pack a snack, and it's been a while since lunch."

Ruby reached to tickle his daughter's toes. "Are you hungry?"

Maggie burst into tears.

He was so distracted he almost didn't see the dark shadow run out from the shrubs at the edge of the road—and right in front of his horse.

The horse reared and the buggy lurched. Maggie's sobs were cut off. Mindy cried out.

David pulled back on the reins. The horse stumbled into a pile of brush on the side of the road. It reared again, and there was an audible snap from the buggy.

This time, when David tried to pull back on the reins, he found the tension between the horse's harness and the buggy was all wrong.

Finally, the horse was able to stop at the side of the gravel lane.

"Something ran in front of the horse. Coyote,

maybe." He set the brake and looked over. "Everyone all right?"

Ruby had one hand braced against the passenger door. Her arm was around Mindy, who was pale and wide-eyed.

"I think we are all right." Ruby squeezed Mindy's shoulders and leaned to check on Maggie, whose tears had started up again at an even higher volume.

"It sounded like—did something break on the buggy?" Ruby asked above Maggie's cries.

"I think so. I'm going to get out and check."

He grabbed his flashlight and looked for cars before he got out. It wasn't completely safe to be stranded on the side of the road like this. The buggy had reflectors, but some *Englisher* drivers didn't pay attention, and a dark-colored Amish buggy on the side of the road could be missed at this time of twilight.

One of the shafts had snapped. He could see it even as he approached, careful to talk in a calming voice to the gelding, who was still bobbing his head in the traces. The shaft that connected the horse's harness to the buggy was now in two pieces. One hung low from the body of the buggy while the other dangled from the leather harness attached to the horse.

As David neared, he pointed the flashlight at the horse and saw a gash in the gelding's foreleg. There was blood seeping down the leg, inky against the growing darkness.

"It's all right, friend." He laid his palm on the horse's shoulder, felt the flicker of the animal's skin beneath his hand.

He knelt to examine the horse and could hear the cadence of Ruby's voice speaking inside the buggy. Maggie's cries had quieted some. The woods were nearly silent, only a lone cricket chirping.

Something rustled in the bushes off the side of the road. Maybe the same something that had frightened his horse?

David crouched by the horse and shone his flashlight through the horse's legs to the brush beyond. He couldn't see anything moving but gave a shout anyway.

Silence.

The door of the buggy banged open, and then Ruby called out, "Mindy, stay here."

He straightened and turned because he already knew that his daughter wasn't going to listen. He caught Mindy as Ruby followed her out of the buggy. Ruby stumbled on the step and grabbed the front wheel to steady herself.

"I'm sorry." Ruby was breathing hard. "She got away from me."

He shook his head, one hand on top of Mindy's head. "You're not a babysitter or a nanny tonight."

Mindy pointed at the horse, tugging on his hand. She'd already seen the injury, and her face crumpled.

"He's going to be all right," David said. "We'll get him home and doctor him right up."

But he looked back at the buggy, the broken shaft. Maggie started wailing from inside.

They were at least a mile from his home and would have to trudge through the dark to get there. It couldn't be more obvious that they weren't going to make it to dinner.

David went quiet, staring at the horse in the growing dark. He had to be frustrated or flustered by what had happened. Mindy stood at his side, still tugging him toward the injured horse.

Maggie's cries were making Ruby's skin prickle.

"Is there somewhere we can go?" Ruby asked quietly.

Her words seemed to galvanize him. "Yes. We're about a mile from my home. My parents live next door, and they've got a buggy I can borrow. After we get him taken care of." He nodded to the horse.

The horse favored its left front leg and made agitated *whuffles* from deep in its chest.

"Can you help me unhitch the horse?"

Ruby hesitated. "I would rather not."

In the low light, she could see his brows scrunch over his eyes. "Are you afraid of horses?"

It wasn't something that came up in casual conversation. She supposed if they were going forward with the three dates—and more—he deserved to know. "I was badly bitten by one of our horses when I was a little girl. I can drive a buggy... I just prefer not to have to hitch it up. Or unhitch it."

He sighed. "I'm sorry to have to ask this, but I'll need your help. The way that shaft is broken, the harness isn't going to come off easily. And I would rather not spook him and have him injure himself worse."

She really didn't want to, but Maggie's cries had somehow grown even louder, and Ruby realized they'd have to stay out here on the side of the road longer if she didn't help.

She tried to swallow back her fear. It didn't help. "O-okay."

David motioned her to come closer to him and the horse. He didn't even seem to remember Mindy was attached to his hand, but an image of Mindy being trampled by the horse played in her mind.

"Mindy, can you go and cheer up Maggie?" she asked, the words wobbly.

"*Goot* idea." David gave his daughter a little push.

Mindy went and hopped up into the buggy.

"He's a gentle one." Maybe he was trying to reassure her, but—

"Then why is he so restless?"

"Because he's hurt. Can you hold his halter?"

Heart beating wildly, she stepped beside David and took hold of the leather strap beside the horse's jaw. Her hand was shaking. It would only take one turn of the horse's head and those giant teeth—

David's hand covered hers, warm and large. Steady. "He's not going to bite you."

"Y-you can't know that."

"I've had him since he was a yearling. We've been working together a long time, haven't we?" David spoke to the horse now as he ran one hand down the animal's shoulder.

The horse calmed, though his ears still flicked back and forth.

And Ruby calmed, too. Enough for David to move away and begin unbuckling the harness. How could he be so calm when she felt anything but?

Was it because he worked with horses every day?

"Have you ever been bitten?"

He moved slowly down the horse's back, unbuckling. "Coupla times. Been stepped on. Kicked."

"You're certainly selling it. Maybe I'll become a farrier."

He chuckled. "Never by this gelding. He's as sweet as they come." He walked around the horse's head to her. "All right. I've got him now. Do you mind getting Maggie out of the buggy?"

"*Ja.* I'll get her."

They walked in the dark, David's flashlight shining a path a little off the road so they wouldn't be in danger of any cars hitting them. Mindy clutched David's hand while Ruby held Maggie. The baby was still fussing, rubbing her face with her tiny fists.

The walk to reach David's home seemed longer than it actually was because of the fussy baby in her arms.

David hesitated in the drive, then pointed to the front porch with the flashlight. "The front door is unlocked. I need to get the gelding's gash covered before it gets infected. Could you—"

"Take the girls inside? *Ja.* Of course. Come on, Mindy. You can show me around."

But Mindy hung close to David's side.

He sighed. "She can stay with me."

"No." The word was out, a sharp sound in the darkness. Ruby blinked away the image of that horse biting or stepping on Mindy. Cleared her throat. "Shouldn't she come inside? Aren't you hungry, little one?"

Mindy stuck close to David's leg, and Maggie's wails got louder. Did she realize they were home?

"Here. So you can find the light inside." David pressed the flashlight into Ruby's hand. "It's…" He hesitated. "It's probably a mess."

Ruby had no choice but to swallow the bad feeling in her throat about Mindy going to the barn and turned to walk up the porch steps. David and Mindy and that horse disappeared around the corner of the house.

This wasn't what she'd expected tonight. She'd thought maybe David would bring the girls along, and he had. But she couldn't have imagined Mindy's stubbornness or Maggie's upset.

Ruby entered through the front door and shone the beam of light around. There was a lamp. She lit it, and soft light suffused the room. Books and blocks were scattered on the floor. Stairs led up to a second floor, and the kitchen was through a doorway beyond.

Ruby went there.

Dishes from lunch covered the table. Bowls on the counter looked as if they'd had cereal for breakfast. Her face warmed at the thought that David wouldn't have wanted her to see this.

She went to the fridge, Maggie still on her hip. Her little fist was in her mouth now.

"Oh, poor *boppli*. You're so hungry you are eating your hand."

Ruby found a large bowl covered in tinfoil that contained homemade noodles with chicken. That was good enough for now. She took it out of the fridge, closing the door with her hip as she balanced the girl on her other side. She went to the counter and began rummaging under the cabinets for a pot to heat up the food in.

She didn't know where David kept everything, and it took her three tries to find the cabinet with pots stacked neatly inside.

Once she'd gotten the noodles warming on the stove, she settled a snuffling Maggie in the high chair at the table. She found a loaf of bread on the counter and tore a piece in half to give to her, and Maggie picked it up and shoved it into her mouth. Ruby began clearing the dishes, moving them to the counter near the sink.

Through the window, she could see light shining from a barn door across the yard. A shadow moved through the triangle of light, still inside the barn.

She started running hot water in the sink in preparation to wash the dishes. There was a sticky spot on the floor beneath her feet. Maybe she should take care of that, too.

Was this what it would be like if she married David? Him working long hours while she cared for the girls? Cleaned the house?

It wasn't that different from what Lily wanted, was it?

Maggie made her "yah, yah, yah" sound, and

Ruby went to the stove to check on the noodles. They were warm without being hot, and she quickly put some in a bowl and moved to sit at the table to feed them to Maggie.

"Who's a hungry girl?" she cooed.

Maggie gave her a lopsided smile. Her face was still tearstained and mottled red, but she chewed the bite Ruby spooned into her mouth. She seemed happier. For now.

"Wonder if your sister is hungry," Ruby murmured. Mindy *must* be as hungry as Maggie, but she'd wanted to go to the barn.

She remembered the way David had caught Mindy in his arms out there on the road. Protective, strong. He'd kept her safe. He would do the same in the barn.

Ruby glanced around the kitchen again, seeing it with new eyes. David was doing his best. He'd been embarrassed for her to see the house, chagrined that things had happened and the date hadn't gone as planned.

He needed help. He needed a partner.

And looking at Maggie's dear face, Ruby knew the girls needed a mother.

Chapter Seven

Ruby finished wiping the lower half of Maggie's face with a warm, wet washcloth. The toddler had finished her dinner, but her cheeks were still flushed, and she remained fussy, totally different than the gentle girl Ruby had played with earlier in the week. Ruby suspected she was teething.

But she didn't know whether David wanted the little one to take some medicine or if he had something for her to chew on. And David and Mindy were still in the barn.

She picked up Maggie from the high chair. They bopped their way to the kitchen window. The barn was still lit from the inside.

"What do you think they're doing out there?" She knew the girl couldn't answer. But Maggie laid her head on Ruby's shoulder, still snuffling.

"Poor little one." She slowly meandered through the kitchen and into the living room.

It was cozy. Lived in. On one wall was a book-shelf. Across the top were novels and nonfiction, and on the bottom shelves were children's books. Looking at that shelf made her heart warm.

Two couches took up spaces catty-corner on the two walls away from the front door. She sort of thought the arrangement made too much open space across the floor. She would've put the two couches in the center of the room facing each other. A rocking chair sat in the far corner tucked next to the staircase. Almost pushed aside. Her stomach twisted. Had it belonged to David's wife? Had he tried to push thoughts of her, his grief, aside just like the chair?

She eyed the stairs and thought about looking for Maggie's bedroom. It was surely getting close to her bedtime. It wouldn't take much to put her in a nightgown and change her diaper.

But while David had told her she could go inside, he probably didn't want her snooping around his house. Right?

She had made quick work of the dishes while Maggie ate, pacing back and forth from the sink to the table to check on the girl. She still had the pot warming on the stove so Mindy and David could eat. Her stomach was growling, too, but she wanted to make sure there was enough.

Pacing back into the kitchen, she tried to get Maggie to settle. The girl restlessly turned her face this way and that, never seeming to get comfortable. She still had her hand in her mouth.

Finally, two shadows separated from the barn and moved toward the house. She bounced Maggie around the kitchen as she became more unhappy.

Ruby heard the murmur of David's voice as the back door opened. "I'm sorry it took so long. He was cut in two places—" He stopped short, one hand on Mindy's shoulder as he caught sight of Ruby holding Maggie.

"She's still crying," David said.

Mindy watched with wide, serious eyes.

Ruby smoothed Maggie's hair from her warm, damp forehead. "I think she has a low fever. And she may be teething. She keeps chewing on her hand."

In only a few minutes, Maggie had soaked the shoulder of Ruby's dress with drool.

"Teething?" She could almost feel David's concern rise as he crossed the floor to the sink to wash up.

"Has she been fussy all day?"

"I don't know," he said over the running water. "She didn't eat as much as usual at breakfast or lunch, but I didn't think…"

His words trailed off as he cut off the water and picked up a towel to dry his hands.

Maggie was fussing in earnest now, and Ruby

felt movement near her side just before Mindy hugged her around the leg. Ruby shifted her weight so she was better balanced.

Mindy pushed her face into Ruby's skirt, her shoulders now shaking.

Ruby glanced at David, who had noticed everything even as he'd walked toward her.

There was some shadow in his expression as he reached for Maggie. The girl held out her little arms to him with a sad gurgle.

He settled her against his chest, one hand cupping her head. He must've felt how warm she was, because he exhaled sharply.

"I meant to ask my father to walk over and watch the girls while I take you home," David said quietly. "But that will have to wait."

"Yes, of course." She knew he needed to see Maggie settled first.

He looked chagrined, his gaze on the floor. "This isn't what I'd hoped tonight would be like."

"What did you want it to be like?"

He rocked Maggie slightly in his arms, flustered by her question. "I don't know." His glance flicked to his older daughter. "C'mon, Mindy. Let's go upstairs to bed."

Mindy shook her head, her arms still around Ruby's waist.

Ruby's arm came around the girl's shoulders. "She didn't eat her supper yet," she said, reminding David. Ruby's stomach growled as if to punctuate the statement.

Surprise and dismay flickered across his expression. His gaze darted to the staircase behind Ruby, and he shifted his feet.

"It's fine," Ruby reassured him. "Take Maggie up to bed."

She settled Mindy at the table with a bowl of noodles and chicken and then made herself a bowl when her hunger became too much to bear. There was still enough for David, too. His she left on the stove.

She could hear his footsteps creaking on the second floor as she and Mindy ate. The girl was not as animated as she had been before. Maybe she had picked up on the tension between Ruby and David. Children were intuitive that way.

Whether or not things worked out with Ruby's far-fetched plan, she didn't want the girl to be worried. Ruby cleared away her bowl.

Mindy finished the last of her food and was out of the chair before Ruby had enough time to give any instruction. Mindy carefully picked up her plate and fork and held it in front of her in a way that let Ruby know she knew what to do. She set it on the counter next to where Ruby was washing up her bowl, Mindy's expression grave and her eyes serious.

All Ruby could see was a little girl who must want to please her father. "Thank you, Mindy."

Mindy beamed at the faint praise.

The girl stood at Ruby's side while she finished. Ruby dried her hands on a dish towel. Mindy scampered off, and Ruby felt a pinch of uncertainty. She didn't want the girl to run upstairs and interrupt David as he settled Maggie, who desperately needed sleep.

But Mindy skipped back in the room before Ruby could go after her. She carried a flat square book in her hands and presented it to Ruby with a pleading expression.

"You want me to read you a story?"

Mindy nodded, unsmiling.

Ruby let Mindy take her by the hand and lead her into the living room. Straight to the rocker that had been pushed into the corner. It was clear that it had been unused for a while, because the rocker rested against the wall in a way that would scratch it unless it was moved.

Ruby dragged it away from the wall.

She sat down, and before she'd settled her skirts around her, Mindy clambered into her lap and leaned against Ruby. As she began to read, Mindy curled even closer and tipped her head to lean against Ruby's shoulder.

Here was more proof that the girls needed a mother.

The question was, would David see it the same way? If he didn't, how could she prove it to him?

David paused at the top of the stairs, listening for sounds of Ruby and Mindy from below.

Ruby must be right about the teething. Normally good-natured, Maggie had been inconsolable and had finally fallen asleep on his shoulder. She had stirred when he put her down but finally settled after he had rested his hand on her back in the crib.

Ruby had been right about his daughter. She had been nervous about Mindy helping him in the barn, and he'd overridden her concern. He'd disappeared on her, then came back to find her cradling his fussing daughter. Her stomach had growled.

He certainly hadn't made a good impression.

But even though Maggie had been crying, Ruby had been patient and loving with her.

It was so still in the house. Where were Ruby and Mindy?

He moved down the stairs quietly, listening for any sound. When his feet hit the bottom step, he felt a change in the air.

Ruby was there, sitting in the corner in Jessica's old rocking chair. Mindy was on her lap, and there was a book tucked in the chair beside them. Mindy must have drifted off while they'd been reading. Mindy looked completely content, her face peaceful in sleep. He knew from personal experience that if Ruby's arm wasn't already asleep, it would be soon, judging by the way it was tucked under Ruby's head, keeping the little girl from giving herself a crick in the neck.

First, Ruby had taken care of Maggie. Now she'd cared for Mindy.

His stomach rumbled, reminding him that he hadn't done anything to alleviate Ruby's hunger.

"There are leftovers on the stove," she whispered.

He hesitated between the chair and the kitchen. "Did you eat?"

He was relieved when she nodded. He hadn't meant for any of this to go the way it had.

"You should eat."

Mindy needed to be tucked into her own bed, but he was afraid the girl would wake when he tried to move her. He looked from the staircase toward the kitchen and finally decided to listen to Ruby. Moving Mindy could wait a few minutes.

He went into the kitchen but stopped short. Someone—Ruby—had done the dishes. And it looked like she'd wiped down the counter, too. His feet carried him to the stove, where there was, indeed, warm food. A clean, empty bowl waited on the counter for him.

The floor wasn't sticky where Maggie had

spilled apple juice this morning and he hadn't had time to properly wipe it up.

Not only had she cared for the girls, but she'd looked after him, too.

His stomach shifted uncomfortably, the same way it had earlier in the buggy when she'd asked about his day.

It had been a long time since anyone had taken care of him. Not since Jessica died.

He had forgotten what it felt like.

He ate his food in silence, devouring it without really tasting it. His thoughts whirled and spun. He'd agreed to Ruby's three dates, but he'd done so thinking that nothing would convince him to get married again.

But tonight, having her here to help had made things smoother. If he'd been alone with the girls and the accident had happened, he'd have struggled to get home.

Ruby had made it easy.

But he still couldn't reconcile the idea of marrying again. He couldn't go back to that dark place he'd been in after Jessica's death.

He didn't have answers.

He washed up his plate and returned to the living room. Ruby was fishing the book out from beside her, where it had tucked into the chair. He took it from her and looked down at it.

It was a familiar one. Something Jessica had often read to Mindy. Grief hit hard.

"You must read to her a lot," Ruby whispered. "She loves that book."

He shook his head. Cleared his throat. "I don't."

Her mother did.

Ruby leaned her cheek against Mindy's head. "You should."

There's not enough of me, his thoughts chattered through his head.

Before he could say anything, Mindy stirred.

Ruby opened and closed her fist. He'd known her arm would fall asleep.

"I'll get her in bed," he said.

But when he tried to take Mindy out of Ruby's lap, the girl shifted so her arms were around Ruby's neck.

Ruby stood up, forcing him to step back. "I can carry her if you'll show me her room."

The house had been built half a century ago, and the stairs were narrow and steep. David stayed close beside Ruby in case she needed help navigating them.

They'd just reached the shadowed turn near the second-floor landing, and her toe must have nicked the top of one of the stairs, because Ruby wobbled on her feet. He saw it happen and clamped his arm behind her onto the banister.

His other arm came around her waist, and he pulled her into his body as he steadied them both.

He wasn't prepared for the softness of her arm pressing against his sternum or the way she seemed to fit neatly against him. The hair at her temple brushed against his jaw, and he got a waft of scent. Something light and flowery and womanly. It was completely different from the way Jessica used to smell, and for a moment, he was startled and tensed.

"All right?" His voice was low so he wouldn't wake Mindy.

Ruby nodded, the movement of her head brushing her hair against him again. He swallowed hard and let her go.

He was off-kilter from her nearness, and he didn't like feeling that way.

Once they'd cleared the last stair, he pointed her to the doorway on the right, then waited for her to go so he could put some distance between them.

What was that?

He'd been completely unprepared for the attraction that had bloomed inside him.

Inside the bedroom, he was careful to keep several feet between them.

Against one wall, Maggie was already asleep in her crib. Ruby moved to the narrow bed near the opposite wall beneath the window and bent to gently lay Mindy in it.

Somewhere along the way, probably downstairs, she'd already removed Mindy's shoes and socks and apron, and now the girl wore only her dress. He didn't care about changing her into her nightgown. He wanted Mindy to be able to rest after an eventful evening.

He moved to the end of the bed, prepared in case Mindy woke up discombobulated as Ruby gently disentangled herself.

Mindy stirred, reaching for Ruby. "Don't leave."

He froze at the barely audible whisper from his daughter. Ruby's startled gaze snapped to him in the moonlight streaming through the window.

Mindy had spoken.

He couldn't believe it.

Ruby settled one hand to rub gentle circles on Mindy's back. "I'm here, little one."

Mindy didn't stir again and drifted off to sleep.

They waited a long time before he nodded toward the door, and they both tiptoed out.

He couldn't contain his whirling thoughts as he followed Ruby down the stairs.

Mindy had spoken.

His father was pushing through the front door as they reached the living room.

"I saw the lights on."

Daed stopped short, staring at Ruby.

David hadn't told him he was taking her on a date. Why would he?

Daed's expression shuttered as David explained.

"If Maggie's not feeling well, I can take your date home," *Daed* mumbled.

He would?

David had planned to drive Ruby home himself, but maybe *Daed* was right. If Maggie woke, she'd want David and only David.

"It's fine," Ruby said quietly before he came to a decision.

He didn't know whether or not to believe her, but he didn't seem to have much choice.

With *Daed* watching, he didn't even clasp her hand. He probably should have hugged her.

Mindy spoke!

But he couldn't shake the remembrance of the attraction that had felt like an attack, and instead they shared an awkward goodbye.

Was this a turning point for Mindy?

It was Ruby she'd wanted. Not him.

What did that mean? For all of them?

Chapter Eight

David unbuckled the thick leather strap that held his horse to the special wagon he used when he was out shoeing horses. He smoothed his hand over the animal's shoulder, promising with his touch that he'd bring some grain in a bit.

His gelding was still healing from the gash it had received days ago. His friend Will had loaned him the use of his horse, a bay mare. David used the horse's halter to guide it out from between the two shafts and into the barn.

"Here we go, old girl."

The mare headed straight for the food trough, and David didn't close her in the stall. He got out the currycomb and used it to go over every inch of the horse as the mare devoured her supper.

David's stomach growled. Instead of reminding him to eat, the sound reminded him of Ruby's growling stomach from their disaster of a date three days ago.

She hadn't been far from his mind since.

The barn door creaked as it opened, and he looked up to see *Daed* walk inside. David nodded a hello as he put away the currycomb and returned to check the mare's hooves.

"The girls all right?" David asked.

Daed nodded.

"And *Mamm*?"

"She's *goot*. Everyone is *goot*."

David squatted and pulled the mare's right foreleg into the cradle of his thighs. There was a tiny pebble caught in the frog, and he needed to remove it.

His *mamm* had insisted on keeping the girls today. She'd felt well enough to walk over to David's house yesterday evening to tell him herself, and she'd looked pink-cheeked and hale.

But he'd still worried all day. He certainly wasn't back to normal, whatever that was, and he didn't know whether he ever could be.

Daed must have something to say, or he wouldn't have come over. Impatience bubbled. Horses were so much easier than people.

David had finished examining all four of the mare's hooves by the time *Daed* snapped one of his suspenders.

"Are you seeing that girl?"

"Her name is Ruby." *Daed* knew her name. David had mentioned her several times. Including the fact that Ruby had gotten Mindy to speak. The sleepy whisper had ignited all of David's hopes. His chatterbox was still inside her somewhere.

But there'd been no more words despite the many prayers he'd sent heavenward.

He'd been foolish, hoping and praying for Mindy to talk to him. She'd spoken to Ruby. It was Ruby she'd asked for in colorful crayon drawings. A stick-figure Mindy and Ruby, always wearing a blue dress.

"Your *mamm* is better," *Daed* said, and it took a moment for David's thoughts to track.

Mamm was better, which meant she could watch the girls.

"You don't have to marry again. Or at least you've got no reason to rush." *Daed* stood with one hand on the nearest stall, his gaze piercing but giving nothing away.

Marry.

The word tossed David back to that moment when Ruby had stumbled on the stairs, the feel of her in his arms, the way she'd smelled.

The way his heartbeat had sped up.

"Just because *Mamm* is better now doesn't mean she won't get sick again."

"We'll make do," *Daed* said stubbornly. "Family takes care of family."

David frowned. "What if *Mamm* is the one

who needs caring for?" He couldn't forget how pale she'd been before Doc had gotten her meds adjusted.

Daed was silent. David couldn't help wondering what had prompted this conversation.

"Maybe I'm lonely," David blurted, surprising them both.

That wasn't the point. It wasn't about him anymore. It was about the girls. Where had those words even come from?

He didn't dwell on being lonely. He was too busy, caught up in caring for Mindy and Maggie or the day-to-day needs of his job.

But he'd felt a pang, hadn't he? As if Ruby had pressed on a bruise when she'd left him a plate warming on the stove. She had anticipated his needs, thought of him.

He tried to tell himself he didn't need someone taking care of him, but he also couldn't stop remembering how she'd gone about it. If only he had a brother or sister to lean on, maybe he'd feel differently. But he didn't say that out loud.

Daed moved away, signaling the conversation was over. David wanted to call after him, demand he deliver the advice that David needed. Validate his feelings.

But he didn't.

And *Daed* didn't turn around.

David finished cleaning and putting away his tools for the day, praying for patience and wisdom.

He went next door to his parents' house and stopped in the mudroom to wash up. Even over the faucet running, he could hear Maggie's happy babbles. And nothing from Mindy.

How long would she make him wait to hear her voice again?

He found the girls in the kitchen playing with salt dough at the table, Maggie in the high chair. *Mamm* was at the stove stirring a pot of homemade mac and cheese.

"*Goot* evening." David leaned over and kissed Mindy's cheek first, then Maggie's, earning a giggle from the toddler as he blew a raspberry into her shoulder.

He crossed the room to kiss *Mamm's* cheek, too, earning a pleased protest.

When *Mamm* glanced over her shoulder at him, her eyes creased with concern. "What's the matter?"

"You look tired." David avoided her question.

"Of course I do. I've been chasing these two around all day. I'm all right." And *Mamm* certainly seemed so. Maybe the medicine the doctor had prescribed was working. "Did your father say something?"

David snorted. "He never does." He moved to grab a mug out of an upper cabinet across the room and then walked back to the stove, where the coffeepot was warming.

"He's worried you're rushing into, um, things—" she glanced over her shoulder at the girls "—with Ruby."

David choked on the first sip of his coffee.

Marriage. She meant rushing into marriage.

He coughed to clear his throat, and once that had subsided, he ran a hand over his mouth and jaw.

"Is that what you think?"

Mamm's gaze cut to him. She had a way of seeing right through him—always had. "I want to see you happy again. If she makes you happy, then…"

That wasn't an answer.

"You knew right from the start, with Jessica," *Mamm* said, moving to pull bowls from the cabinet.

This isn't like that. He bit back the words, sipping his coffee again as an excuse to think before he spoke.

Falling for Jessica had been effortless, and he really hadn't had a choice. It had happened the first time he'd seen her.

He liked Ruby well enough, but he wasn't looking for love again. Would probably turn tail and run if he came face-to-face with it again. He couldn't afford to lose someone he loved again. It hurt too much. His grief was still fresh.

He didn't have an answer for *Mamm and* suspected she wouldn't like that he was considering marriage like a business deal. Instead, he went to the table and sat in one of the empty chairs.

"What are you making?"

"Yah, yah, yah." Maggie banged her fists on the table.

He didn't expect Mindy to answer, but she held out her creation on the palm of her hand.

"Is it a bird?" He could see the shape of it—maybe. Was that a beak?

Mindy nodded, her face lighting up.

Don't go. He heard her whisper again, clear as day.

Mindy wanted Ruby.

And he wanted the old Mindy back. He wasn't enough for her on his own, but he could marry Ruby, and she could bring Mindy back.

Maybe he could marry Ruby.

He winced to think that he'd let so much time elapse since their date. He hadn't reached out, though he'd been on a call close to her family's farm only yesterday. He could've delivered a note or even stopped by to see if she was home.

Had he waited too long?

"Do you know David Weiss?"

Ruby glanced up in surprise. She was clearing

the now-empty plate from her customer's table. Her *Englisher* customer.

Why was he asking about David?

"He's the local farrier," she said.

The man narrowed his eyes. Just a little.

Up until now, she hadn't paid much attention to him. He seemed like any other customer. He wore a T-shirt and jeans. Glasses. He'd been paying most of his attention to a tablet, swiping and tapping. But now his gaze seemed pointed somehow.

"I'm an old friend," he said.

Skepticism rose inside her, but she worked to mask it in her expression. She didn't want to lose the tip he might leave by being rude.

She hadn't spent much time with David. Not enough to know whether he had many *Englisher* friends. But something, some stirring in her gut, was telling her to tread carefully here.

"Do you know where I could find him?" the *Englisher* asked.

"He might be at home." Ruby picked up the silverware and reached for his empty glass.

"And where is that?"

She smiled, but it felt stretched and unnatural. If this man was an old friend, why didn't he know where David lived? She knew enough to be cautious. Sometimes *Englishers* were too curious about the Amish people. And she wasn't going to tell him where to find David if he didn't already know.

She shrugged and smiled. "I'll bring some change." She picked up the cash and the ticket he'd left on the edge of the table.

Maybe he wouldn't tip at all, since she hadn't told him David's address, but she couldn't find it in her to divulge that information.

She dropped off his change while carting a tray of food to another table so she wouldn't have to stop and speak to him. He left soon after.

What a strange interaction. Ruby was still mulling it over when Naomi stepped in shoulder-to-shoulder with her at the drink station.

"Did you hear?" Naomi whispered.

It was on the tip of Ruby's tongue to tell her she didn't want to gossip when Naomi rushed on, "Emma's getting married. She gave her notice today."

Ruby murmured some acknowledgement and took the pitcher of water to refill customer drinks.

She needed to find Lovina. They could commiserate together.

But when her tables had finally cleared of customers and she found Lovina stocking cans of jams and jellies at the front of the restaurant, Lovina barely glanced at her.

"I guess you'll be giving yours soon enough."

A bitter undertone to the words set Ruby back. "What are you talking about?"

Lovina kept stacking jars on the shelf. "I saw you with David Weiss after church last Sunday. You were talking out in the parking area, near his buggy. You looked very cozy."

Oh.

Ruby didn't know if her expression softened or what Lovina saw on her face, but Lovina's features tightened as if she was hiding her hurt. She looked down at the box at her feet. "I guess sharing an apartment was a bad idea."

"It wasn't," Ruby said quickly. "But…your other idea was better."

Lovina was in profile to her, but she saw when the words registered. The next jar Lovina put on the shelf clanked against its neighbor, the sound jarring. "I guess all that talk about never having a perfect match was nonsense, then."

Hurt swelled. "No, it wasn't. This—if anything happens between me and David, it won't be a love match."

She couldn't tell Lovina about their agreement. Not now, not when her friend was saying hurtful things. Lovina wouldn't understand.

And she didn't even know if the agreement still stood. It had been four days without a word from the man who'd been in her thoughts almost constantly. *The girls*, she corrected her wayward thoughts. The girls had been on her mind constantly.

Lovina frowned and stared at Ruby. "How do you know you're not making a mistake? Maybe Jonathan wasn't your perfect match either."

Lovina's words were like a hot knife slicing into her tender heart. Ruby had told Lovina about her losses in confidence, believing they shared a similar grief. But Lovina was using her knowledge like a weapon right now, and Ruby felt as if she was bleeding inside. She couldn't find words. "My *mamm*—"

Lovina interrupted. "Marriage isn't for everyone. I realized that after Silas walked away from me. What if your *mamm* was wrong? What if there's not a perfect match for you out there?"

"Jonathan was my match," Ruby said stubbornly.

"You were both young when he died," Lovina argued. "What if things changed as you both got older? What if you didn't even like him?"

Lovina was being absurd. And it was as if she was attacking *Mamm* and everything Ruby had known since her childhood.

"Just because you're bitter and alone doesn't mean you have to try to sabotage my happiness." Ruby inhaled sharply, the air getting caught in her chest, making it ache.

She hadn't meant to say that. Hadn't meant

to get so angry, so defensive. Lovina's expression had closed off, other than the angry frown she wore.

I'm sorry. The words caught behind Ruby's sternum.

Something snagged Lovina's attention over Ruby's shoulder. She turned to see David standing in the entryway, the open door letting in a cool fall breeze and backlighting him so that the breadth of his shoulders was visible. Her stomach twisted with happiness at seeing him mixed with heartbreak over the disagreement with Lovina.

She said nothing to her friend and went to meet him. She couldn't read his expression. He was alone. The girls were nowhere to be seen.

"Are you here for supper?" She still felt off from the argument with Lovina but tried to find a smile for him.

"I'm here for you." His words might have been romantic if they hadn't been delivered with such a serious expression. He wore no hint of a smile.

That didn't stop her stomach from dipping low.

"I think we should try that second date." He glanced behind Ruby. She didn't have to turn to know Lovina was still crouched near the hostess stand. Was her friend watching?

"I didn't know whether you were working tonight."

"Umm, I'm finished in about five minutes. Do you want to eat here?"

He glanced around the restaurant, shook his head. "I had something else in mind, if that's all right with you."

Relief flooded her. She didn't know if she could manage to eat a thing under Lovina's angry, watchful gaze.

"I'll finish up here and clock out with my boss."

Lovina was conspicuously silent as Ruby squatted next to her, intending to finish stocking the jams and jellies.

"You should just go." The bitter undertone to Lovina's words was back.

Emotion swelled in Ruby's chest. She didn't want to leave things unfinished with the box of jellies—or with her friend. But Lovina wouldn't even look at her, and David was waiting. So she left, trying to catch her breath and find her bearings as she moved through the near-empty dining room to clock out and fetch her things. How could she focus on David when she felt so discombobulated?

She would put what had happened with Lovina out of her mind. For now. And later, when she'd had time to think and make sense of what had happened, she would make things right with her friend.

Chapter Nine

David was nervous.

He'd thought about this date, about what he would say, nonstop since he'd left *Mamm* and *Daed's* house last night.

Ruby had been quiet after they'd left the restaurant. He had sensed some tension between her and the other waitress—he couldn't remember her name—when he'd come inside.

Was that why Ruby was pensive?

He didn't know how to break the awkward silence. It was easier with the girls present. But he also needed to know this was going to work between the two of them. Whether they could be friends. Because some day, Mindy and Maggie would grow up and get married, and he and Ruby would still be together.

If they got married, it would be forever.

"Where are the girls tonight?" Ruby finally broke the silence.

"At home. My *mamm* has been feeling much better lately, and she and *Daed* came over to stay with them for a few hours."

"I'm glad your *mamm* is better."

"*Ja*, me, too." But it was hard to forget how pale her face had been, how frail she'd seemed that afternoon weeks ago. What if the medicine stopped working?

"Someone was asking about you in the restaurant today."

He looked at her and was captured by the beauty of her profile as she glanced out the glass protector at the front of the buggy.

It took him a moment to play back her words in his memory. "Someone needs their horse shod?"

"No. He said he was an old friend, but he was dressed like an *Englisher*. Acted like one, too. I told him I hadn't seen you in a few days. Which I hadn't. Then."

She smiled mischievously, and the curve of her lips made his heart kick against his ribs. Her eyes danced, and his pulse wanted to join in.

He glanced forward, pretended he needed his full attention on the road, though there weren't any turn-offs and his horse was reliable.

Why did he suddenly feel out of breath? He could feel every fiber of his shirt against his skin, the weight of the reins on his palms seemed heavier. He'd felt attraction before. When he'd first begun courting Jessica, he'd been drawn to her. His pulse had raced, just like it was now.

But Ruby didn't think of him like that. She wanted this marriage for the girls' sake and for her own reasons.

He must control himself. He wouldn't fall in love again. No matter how much his heart went pitter-patter.

The silence grew uncomfortable in the buggy again until she asked, "Where are we going?"

"Here." He turned the buggy into the drive for a local college.

"Ooh, are we attending a lecture?"

She sounded excited.

"I suppose you like lectures? What topics?"

"All topics. I love to learn."

Since it was evening, there was very little traffic. He spotted a parking area full of cars and turned the buggy in. He parked the buggy in a grassy area beneath a large elm.

"All topics except horses?" he teased gently.

She wrinkled her nose at him.

"I'm sorry to disappoint you, but it isn't a lecture tonight. If you'll give me a minute to settle the horse…?"

She made her own way out of the buggy as he tied off the horse and fetched the picnic blanket and a large basket out of the storage compartment.

"Another picnic?" She fell into step beside him

as they moved through the parking lot and onto a grassy field beyond.

"Sort of."

As they crossed the grass, now turning yellow before it went dormant for winter, the sound of instruments being tuned wafted over the light evening breeze. Good. They'd made it in time.

"Is it a concert? A musical?"

He leveled a look on her. "How is it you don't like surprises?"

She shrugged, a shadow flitting behind her eyes. "I don't know. I never have."

"It's an orchestra concert put on by the college band." He looked up at the sky, where clouds were gathering on the far horizon. "It's an out-door amphitheater. Hopefully the weather will hold off."

She clasped her hands in front of her. "I love music."

She was adorable. He reminded himself grimly that that was irrelevant. "The girls love music. My—my wife used to sing to them."

"You don't sing?"

"I do. In church."

Her brows were drawn. "But not to the girls?"

Oh. He shook his head. He'd never thought of it. There'd been so little joy after Jessica passed away. He couldn't have found a song inside himself, not even for Mindy or Maggie. Maybe he should've tried harder.

"You'll have to make me a list of some of their favorite songs."

He hadn't realized it until they'd started talking about this, but he couldn't remember the way Jessica's voice had sounded when she sang. Frantic upset had him scouring his memory bank, past the recent thoughts of Ruby's mischievous smile and her cuddling Mindy close, until he caught hold of a fragment of memory. Mentally, he grabbed it and held on until he could see Jessica in his mind's eye, sitting on their bed, singing softly to an infant Mindy held in her arms.

He startled when Ruby asked, "David? Would you make me a list of songs? For the girls?"

"I can't remember them," he said gruffly.

He saw her face fall, but his heart was pounding and he was suddenly sweating. Had he really started to forget his wife? Would he forget pieces of her until there was nothing left?

Ruby stayed quiet, intuitive enough to know that something was wrong.

The amphitheater was in the middle of a grassy knoll, and giant concrete stairs made for sitting on led to a stage and orchestra pit at the bottom. There was plenty of grass surrounding the amphitheater for David to comfortably spread the picnic blanket.

Ruby settled on the quilt, arranging her skirt over her legs curled beneath her. She watched the conductor readying himself at a podium on the stage, carefully keeping her gaze averted.

He put the picnic basket on the blanket between them. Then he moved it so he could sit next to her.

She glanced at him in surprise.

"I'm sorry," he said in a low voice when the first notes of an instrumental piece floated to their ears. "I'm—not good at this. Every conversation seems to be a minefield."

Her gaze shone with compassion or maybe empathy. "Surely we can figure it out together," she whispered.

She had such a kind heart. He released a breath and some of the tension that had gripped him moments before.

The music unfolded around them, and he snuck glances at Ruby as he unloaded things from the picnic basket and made a plate for her. She did love music. Her eyes flitted from performer to performer, and she swayed slightly to the tune he didn't know.

He handed her a plate filled with thick slices of cold ham, cheese and fruit. Her mouth twitched as if she wanted to smile.

"What?"

"I was kind of expecting peanut butter," she whispered. "This is better."

She leaned one hand on the picnic blanket, her plate on her lap. It put her close enough that her shoulder brushed his.

This is better.

Ruby had chattered too much. She'd been nervous without Mindy and Maggie present, and she'd stumbled on David's grief and stomped on it with both feet.

She wanted to ask whether they could start over, but she didn't want to push him to the place inside where his face had darkened with grief and his eyes had gone far off.

So she ate her supper in silence as she listened to the music. The concert went from something lively to something romantic that made her think of long twilight walks together.

And then it shifted again, to something that made her think of spring mornings, seeing the sun again after a long winter and hard work done with family.

The song changed to something tumultuous, and her eyes were drawn to the far horizon where lightning flashed. No thunder was audible. The concert would be over long before the rain arrived—if it didn't dissipate before it got here. Her food was long eaten, and David had methodically packed the plates and cutlery back in the basket.

Notes swirled around her, now a soft, sad melody. It made her think of David. Of his grief.

The music and her thoughts tugged at her heartstrings and waltzed around and around her until she couldn't help herself. She needed something to hold onto.

She reached for the picnic blanket beside her, intending to wrap her fist in it. Instead, her hand connected with David's warm grip.

Shocked, she looked up into his face. Maybe she expected him to move away, but his hand clasped around hers, his grip warm and firm.

She turned her face to the stage, but now she was only pretending to hear the music. All she could think was, *David is holding my hand.* All she could feel was the warmth of his palm against hers, the slide of his fingers as he linked their hands together. Her skin felt too tight over her face, and she felt jumpy—like at the slightest provocation she might slide out of her skin.

Her discombobulated state lasted through three songs. David held her hand the entire time.

And then the conductor thanked everyone for coming. The concert was over.

Ruby was blushing, her face an inferno as she stood and brushed imaginary crumbs off her skirts. Even the air felt heavy and expectant.

When she straightened, David was folding the blanket. He put it over one arm and picked up the basket with his other hand.

"It's early yet. Do you want to walk for a bit? There are paths all over campus."

"Sure. Yes."

She felt so jumpy still that she couldn't face sitting next to him in the buggy. Not yet.

David's affectionate touch had been unexpected. She didn't know what to say or think. And David had been reserved on the drive over, speaking only when she'd spoken first.

Maybe she would have a few quiet moments to gather her thoughts. She fell into step beside David.

But to her surprise, he did speak first. "Were you thinking about him? Your fiancé?"

He meant, was she thinking about Jonathan when she'd started crying. She'd never said Jonathan was her fiancé. David must've assumed as much by what she'd told him before.

But she hadn't been thinking of Jonathan. And there was no way she was going to admit she'd been thinking of David.

"Umm, no."

She sensed him look over at her, but she kept her eyes on the path in front of them.

"But you think of him often?"

"Often enough." Why the curiosity now? Had her tears spurred him on?

"You must miss him."

"I—I guess. Sometimes I wonder whether I miss the idea of him more than anything else." She'd surprised him with her blurted statement. Surprised herself, too. Where had that thought come from?

David shook his head as if he didn't understand.

"We never got our chance," she explained.

"You must've loved him very much."

Had she? A part of her wondered if she had missed the chance for that, as well.

"We were so young. Not even courting yet."

"How young?"

"He was only fourteen when he died." She'd been six months older.

She saw the disbelief as it crossed his expression.

"How do you know you even would've suited?"

"My *mamm*... Mamm was...an unofficial matchmaker, I guess. She matched up some of my cousins. And my brothers. She could predict the one person who would be perfect for you.

"Jonathan was my perfect patch. She told me when I was ten. But he died..."

He waited for her to finish.

It was too difficult to say the words. *She died, too.*

"When did your *mamm* die?" he asked softly.

"A few days before my fifteenth birthday."

Only months after Jonathan.

"And you never wanted to court anyone else?"

This was easier to talk about. She swallowed back the hot knot of tears that always gathered in her throat when she thought of her mother.

"I tried. A couple of different times. Walking home with someone after a social. One young man asked me to go to a singing with him, and I did. But…there was something missing with them."

He exhaled sharply, as if what she said meant something to him. She didn't know what.

"After a while, boys stopped asking…and that was fine with me."

"Until Mindy came along."

"Until Mindy came along. And she made me think that maybe there was a family who needed me." She lifted her eyes to look at him. He'd shifted the blanket under the same arm that held the picnic basket. He watched her with a mix of curiosity and something else she couldn't identify.

And then, a huge thunderclap startled them both. Without any other warning, a deluge of rain descended.

Ruby shrieked at the torrent of cold water now soaking her dress. David grabbed her wrist and tugged her forward. She could barely see through the water streaming in her eyes. But he seemed to have a destination in mind.

Her sodden skirts soon became a hindrance, and she wiggled her arm free of David's grasp so she could use both hands to lift her skirts above her shoes.

"Here!" David shouted above the pelting rain.

She followed him up five wide stairs and beneath an awning for one of the lecture halls. The awning was narrow, and she crowded close to try and escape the downpour.

Unexpectedly, David's arm came around her waist. He tugged her into the shelter of his body, scooting her a scant few inches out of the rain.

"I'm sorry," he spluttered, his face close.

She couldn't help a surprised laugh that bubbled out of her. "I can't believe I hadn't noticed the rain had arrived."

She'd been so caught up in their conversation that she'd been oblivious to the worsening weather.

His gaze narrowed on her mouth with fierce concentration. "When you smile…"

He let his words trail off when she desperately wanted him to finish his sentence. When she smiled, *what*?

His lashes were matted together from the rain. Droplets clung to his whiskers, and now her attention was drawn to his unsmiling lips.

She shivered.

He broke the intense moment when he ducked

his head, and his hat dumped water off the brim right into her face.

"Sorry!" he muttered.

He bobbled the blanket and basket in his arm. "The blanket was folded. Maybe the inside of it is still dry."

He shook out the picnic blanket and found that the inside folds were only damp, not wet. She was surprised when he swung it around her shoulders, tucking the ends beneath her chin. It brought them close again, face-to-face.

"Thank you," she murmured.

He stepped back and took off his hat.

"This wasn't how I expected the night to end up. I wanted to tell you—ask you something."

He seemed flustered, his gaze flitting everywhere but her. Finally, he drew a deep breath and looked right at her.

"I don't need another date. If you're still of a mind, I think we should get married. For Mindy's sake, it should be soon."

Chapter Ten

With her hand on the doorknob, Ruby took one last look around her childhood bedroom.

Her wedding morning had arrived.

This would be the last time she left this room as a single woman.

She could remember *Mamm* kneeling beside her next to the bed, listening to her prayers.

As a preteen, she'd occasionally had a friend over, and they'd played a board game on the floor.

Reading in the window, a stolen few minutes of dawn daylight before chores began for the day.

And these past two weeks, sewing her wedding dress. Beth had helped her with some of the trickier stitching.

She'd missed *Mamm*. It was a task *Mamm* would've done with her if she'd still been alive.

Ruby smoothed the dark blue fabric of her

skirt and the organza apron over it. It had been bittersweet, sewing the gown without her *mamm*.

Was she doing the right thing?

She thought of Mindy. Of someday sewing a wedding gown together for Mindy's wedding. Maggie, too.

And she thought of David. She'd barely seen him during the past two weeks as they'd made preparations for the wedding today. He and the girls had come for supper at the restaurant twice, but she'd been busy with other tables and hadn't been able to sit with them or chat.

Ruby had been invited to supper with David and the girls and his parents. It had been so different from the noisy meals she was used to. The family was smaller, but neither David nor his father spoke much.

Things would be different once the wedding was over and she'd settled in. She was determined to bring joy back to David's household.

And to the man.

She had decided it last night during her prayers. David was still grieving. She wouldn't take that away from him. Theirs wasn't a love match. But she could surely find small ways to brighten his life. She'd enlist the girls' help.

A soft knock at her door startled her, and she opened it.

Daed was there on the other side. "*Goot* morning. Can I come in?"

She let her father inside, and he looked at her. His mouth twitched beneath his beard.

"You look beautiful," he said, his voice a little husky.

She blinked at the sudden moisture in her eyes brought on by his unexpected show of emotion.

He had something bundled in his hands, and she recognized the quilt she'd seen on her parents' bed all through her childhood. Her mother's wedding quilt. It had been a gift from *Mamm's* mother and grandmother. The wedding ring pattern was distinctive and the pastel colors beautiful.

"Your mother would want you to have this."

Ruby's heart rose into her throat. "*Daed*, no."

Her father had put away the quilt not long after *Mamm* had died. The first time Ruby had seen their bed without the quilt on it had been like a missing piece of herself.

"She would have made one for you herself." He pressed the quilt into her trembling hands. "She would've been overjoyed for you. David is a *goot* man, and she wanted your happiness."

The knot in Ruby's throat twisted tighter. Would *Mamm* have stopped this wedding? She would've known David wasn't Ruby's perfect match.

"Take it. It is my gift to you."

"Daed..." The protest died on Ruby's lips as her father handed the quilt to her and then folded her in his arms.

After her mother's death, they hadn't had many emotional moments like these. She'd known her father was there to protect and take care of her, but she'd always been closer to *Mamm*.

And now she was leaving home. She'd have a home of her own with David and the girls. She'd come to visit, but that wasn't the same at all.

Daed let her go, ducking his head and being bashful about the tears he had to wipe away.

"Your husband-to-be is waiting downstairs. Friends are starting to arrive. Do you need another minute to yourself?"

Her heart leaped at the thought of David downstairs.

For the girls. This was happening. She would become David's wife in a little while.

She followed *Daed* downstairs, where David sat in the living room with Mindy and Maggie. When he glanced up and caught sight of her, he stood from the couch, gently sitting Maggie in his place.

She got a good look at the fine black suit he wore. It must be new and was perfectly tailored to him. His hair was gleaming as if he'd just washed it.

He stared at her long enough that she blushed and looked down, self-conscious.

"Look at you," said a female voice from the kitchen, off to the side. Beth with a gentle smile.

Ruby was happy to escape the uncomfortable moment and glanced up at her friend, the only attendant she'd chosen today.

She'd wanted to ask Lovina, but she'd been afraid of hurting her friend. Lovina had barely spoken to her since that evening at the restaurant. And not at all since Ruby's wedding had been announced.

It made her heart hurt. She'd thought their friendship was strong, but it had fractured under the events of the past weeks. Had Lovina only been a kindred spirit because neither of them had expected to marry? Ruby tried to consider what she might've felt if things had been different. If Lovina had been the one to marry for convenience, would Ruby have been hurt? She couldn't say.

Beth entered the room, shaking her out of morose thoughts. "Pretty as the first crocus after winter."

Ruby waved off her sister-in-law's praise, but David cleared his throat, bringing her attention right back to him. "She's right. You look lovely."

If anything, she blushed hotter. "Thank you."

Mindy ran out from behind David and right up

to Ruby. Her eyes were big in her face, and she stopped short of touching the brand-new dress and white apron.

Ruby held out her arms, and Mindy crossed the last inches to hug her legs. Ruby's arms came around the girl's shoulders.

"Only a little while longer," she whispered, "and then we'll be a family."

She hadn't said the words aloud until now, and they brought the lump right back into her throat.

She glanced up to see David watching the hug with that serious intensity of his.

David would be her family, too.

But the way her stomach did a slow flip, her body seemed to realize that what David would be to her was completely different from what Mindy and Maggie would be.

"Do you want to come check on the table decorations with me?" Beth asked Mindy.

The little girl lit up and nodded brightly.

Which left Ruby alone with David and a burbling Maggie.

"Do you need anything?" Ruby asked. "A glass of water?"

She didn't know what to do in these moments that seemed fraught with tension. After their guests arrived, there would be a worship service and sermon, and then she and David would exchange wedding vows before the special lunch was served to everyone in attendance. How much longer?

David shook his head.

Maggie spoke nonsense words from the couch, content where she was.

From where Ruby stood near the stairs, the distance between her and David seemed like a gulf, and she didn't know how to cross it. Or whether she should.

"Are you having second thoughts?"

She was taken aback at his question. "No. Are you?"

He shook his head again, a brief expression of relief crossing his features. He adjusted the cuff of one sleeve. "I don't remember being this nervous when I married Jessica."

He didn't look nervous, only his usual reserved demeanor.

And she thought of the private vow she'd made just this morning. She'd promised herself she would bring him joy. So she stepped forward, crossing the distance between them. She touched his forearm, hoping only to offer him comfort.

"We'll get through this together."

The weather had held, and David sat beside Ruby on a wooden bench set up in the Kauffmans' backyard as the bishop delivered a sermon directed toward the two of them. It would be the only time they would sit together in a service. Ruby's words about getting through this together kept ringing through his mind even as he fought to concentrate on the sermon about sacrificial love.

He was the one who had been through a wedding ceremony before. He had witnessed countless marriages, and surely Ruby must've, too. But it was different when it was your own wedding. When the words were directed at him.

He should've been calm. After all, he already knew what to expect. But he felt like he was nineteen all over again, full of jitters and unsure whether he could really fulfill the vows the bishop would give them soon.

It was all becoming real to him at this moment. Once they said their vows, there would be no turning back. He and Ruby would be linked forever.

He would be expected to sacrifice for Ruby. Be expected to be there for her if she was sick or hurt.

Family takes care of family.

He had made those promises to Jessica. He'd known that promising to care for her also meant caring for her emotions.

Back then, he'd thought he could do it. Promised himself he would never end up like his *daed*, closed off and silent.

But he'd been wrong.

He didn't know how to be enough for Mindy and Maggie.

He didn't turn around to look, but he knew his daughters were sitting with his parents just behind Ruby.

Mindy's grief had stolen her voice, and he still didn't know what to do about it.

He would give Ruby and his girls everything he could. Provide for them physically, ensure they wanted for nothing.

But he couldn't share his heart. He didn't have anything of himself to give.

An unexpected nudge against his foot made him blink, though he was careful not to turn his head. He was supposed to be paying attention.

It came again. It could only be Ruby.

Jessica had always crossed her ankles beneath her skirts, and he hadn't noticed until now, but Ruby must sit the same way, too.

She'd nudged his foot with hers, the action hidden beneath her dress.

Had she somehow sensed his turmoil? Or had it been a complete accident?

It came a third time, the barest brush of her foot against the back of his boot.

He was worrying, and somehow she knew it. She was trying to knock him out of his sorrow.

It worked, because now all he could think of

was how very beautiful she'd been when she had appeared at the bottom of the staircase. The dark blue of her dress accentuated her fair complexion and made her eyes seem even bluer.

Sitting beside her, he could smell her, something flowery and delicate. She would be here from now on, a presence in his life. Right beside him.

He'd made his decision, and deep in his heart, he knew it was the right one for the girls.

He prayed Ruby could be happy. He knew she had unresolved feelings about this Jonathan that was supposed to have been her match. And she'd lost her mother so young. She must still grieve the loss sometimes.

His own mother had folded Ruby in a hug when she had seen her this morning. *Daed* had kept his feelings about the marriage to himself, though in David's mind, he had dared his *daed* to say something the last time they'd been together.

And then the sermon part of the ceremony was over, and the bishop was beckoning David and Ruby to join him and stand in front of the family and friends that had gathered.

When the bishop asked them to clasp their hands together, he realized Ruby's were shaking. Or was it him that was shaking?

She watched him with a steady, calm smile.

"It's all right if you're thinking about Jessica," she whispered. She squeezed his hands.

He hadn't been. Other than a few fleeting moments, he had only been thinking of Ruby. She was all he could see as the bishop asked them to repeat their vows to each other.

Her voice was soft and steady. She wanted this. Wanted to be with him.

And he wanted to be with her.

The realization settled deep inside him, making his voice steady as he repeated the vows.

It was finished before he was ready, and suddenly their friends and family surrounded them, offering hugs and congratulations.

In the midst of it, Ruby's hand snuck into his. Or maybe he'd reached for her. He couldn't be sure. Her fingers slipped through his until their hands were intertwined. Linked.

Just like they were now.

She laughed at something her niece said, and he felt the way his heart pounded in his ears too loudly.

He was surprised by the unexpected reaction, thrown by the blood pumping through him and the way his thoughts muddled.

She smiled up at him, gently and sweetly, and he wanted to kiss her. Someone called out that the wedding meal was ready to be served, and he was grateful for the excuse to look away from her.

What was he thinking? This was supposed to be a convenient marriage. He wasn't supposed to feel anything for Ruby other than friendship.

It had been a blip, he told himself. He was caught up in their wedding ceremony and the memories of Jessica that had surfaced.

It didn't mean anything.

Chapter Eleven

David had thought he was prepared to have Ruby in his house, but it was a different thing walking down the hallway and peering through the open door to her bedroom. It was empty, but seeing her dresses hung on the wall reminded him that this extra bedroom was in use now.

In the bathroom, he tried to ignore the sight of her hairbrush and prayer *kapp* laying neatly on a shelf in the bathroom and made quick work of splashing his face with water and drying off with a towel.

It didn't help the awkwardness he felt as he padded through the quiet house. Things didn't feel *wrong*, exactly, but a different energy buzzed through the walls of the house now that Ruby lived here.

What was he supposed to do with her underfoot? The girls must still be asleep. Downstairs, he found Ruby at the kitchen table reading her Bible.

Jessica had read her Bible every day in their bedroom, sitting in a rocking chair near the upstairs window. The same chair he'd moved to the living room.

Ruby glanced up at him, a soft expression on her face.

It was too much, seeing her doing something so familiar.

He hurried past her through the back door to step into his boots on the porch and head out to the barn.

Ruby wasn't Jessica, he reminded himself as he trudged through the dewy grasses. She wasn't trying to be anyone other than herself. Of course there might be some similarities, some reminders of the wife he'd lost. He just hadn't been ready this morning, he reasoned as he scooped grain for his horse and Will's mare.

He checked the gelding's wound, going so far as to remove the dressing, even though he'd changed it only last night. The gelding was almost healed and restless from the way David had kept him penned. But he needed to make sure the wound healed properly, and he couldn't do that without watching over the horse.

He mucked the stalls. Pitched new hay. He dawdled while looking over his list of customers who were due to have their horses reshod and spent longer than normal fetching eggs out of the chicken coop. When he couldn't put it off any longer, he returned to the house.

The scent of warm coffee greeted him when he stepped inside. He inhaled deeply. It had been a long time since someone had made coffee for him. He left the eggs in their basket on the end of the counter and went to the sink to wash up.

"Thank you for those." Ruby nodded to the eggs. She stood at the stove, toasting bread.

Mindy jumped from the table, where she had toast squares slathered with jam on a plate in front of her. She was still in her nightdress and ran toward him as he dried his hands with a towel.

He saw her reach for him with sticky jam-covered fingers, but he didn't stop her as she wrapped her arms around his leg.

Maggie was strapped into a chair on the other side of the table, happily chewing on her own piece of toast. Jam and drool covered her cheeks and chin.

David dragged his leg with Mindy still attached as he crossed the room to kiss the top of Maggie's head. She chortled and he did it again. Then Mindy let go of him to present the top of her head to him, and he kissed her, too. She beamed up at him.

He caught Ruby's tender smile as she took the toast out of the oven.

Mindy looked between Ruby and David and then patted his leg with one hand while she used the other to point at Ruby.

"What do you need?" he asked. "More toast?"

She shook her head. An emphatic no.

"Jam?" he wondered.

"What about some more juice?" Ruby suggested.

An even more emphatic no before Mindy grabbed his hand and pulled. He allowed himself to be led toward the counter and Ruby. There was nothing else out.

What did Mindy want?

His daughter pointed from him to Ruby.

He shook his head, still unclear on what she wanted.

"Maybe she wants you to eat breakfast," Ruby said.

Another firm shake of the head. Another jab with her finger.

"I don't know what you want." He felt a niggle of frustration. Mindy was usually content to watch and take in everything around her. This was unusual for her to try and communicate something.

Ruby's cheeks had gone pink. "You don't think…?"

She was trying to communicate something to him with her slightly wide eyes and the intent look she delivered, but he only shook his head.

He had no idea.

Ruby bent and quirked her finger at Mindy, who leaned close for Ruby to whisper in her ear. Mindy nodded enthusiastically this time, her eyes dancing.

Ruby must've made a good guess. Ruby, who was pink-cheeked when she straightened.

"What?"

She shook her head, and this time Mindy tugged on her hand.

Ruby sighed. "You gave Maggie a good morning kiss and then Mindy."

He stared at her, uncomprehending.

"She wants you to give me a good morning kiss."

His breath stilled in his chest for a moment as he remembered the errant thought he'd had yesterday during the wedding ceremony. He'd imagined brushing a kiss over her lips.

Mindy watched expectantly, but he saw the hesitation in Ruby's stance.

He wasn't the kind of father who gave his daughters everything they wanted. He could explain why he wasn't going to kiss Ruby.

Or he could just do it. He didn't want to hurt his new wife's feelings, either.

He took one step toward Ruby. She leaned toward him.

He tried to ignore the way his heart sped up as he ducked his head and dropped a kiss on Ruby's hair, just in front of her prayer *kapp*.

Her hand settled on his chest, purely for balance. It was there and gone quickly, and then Ruby turned away to the stove. But not before he saw the blush staining her cheeks.

Mindy clapped her hands together. Ruby wasn't quite looking in his direction.

It was the same kiss he'd given his two daughters. But even that simple affection made him feel things he shouldn't.

Ruby scrambled some eggs and cut up an apple from the bowl on the counter before she joined David and the girls at the table.

He was quiet.

Mindy had discomfited him with her prompt to kiss her. But it couldn't be helped now.

Ruby smiled brightly and tried for a distraction. "I may spend some time today unpacking my things. I might have a surprise in store for a couple of little girls…"

Mindy grinned.

David nodded. "The pantry is pretty bare. I can hitch the buggy for you if you'd like to go to the store later."

"You don't mind?"

He shook his head.

"Should I check with your mother and see whether she needs anything?"

"I'm sure she would love for you to drop by. She probably won't come over herself, doesn't want to interrupt you settling in."

That was thoughtful. While David's parents had welcomed her into the family, Ruby didn't know them well, and it would take some time to adjust to a new dynamic now that she'd become a part of the family.

Maggie wasn't eating anymore, only pushing her scrambled eggs around her plate and then dumping them on the floor when she thought Ruby wasn't watching.

Ruby left her own half-eaten meal and scooped Maggie out of the high chair and took her to the sink to wash the sticky jam from her fingers.

"Is there a certain time you would prefer to have supper?" she asked over her shoulder.

She'd turned toward the table with the baby on her hip when she saw the smile drop from Mindy's face.

"I've fallen behind a bit during these past few weeks. It's not that my customers mind, but some of the horses' feet need tending. I might be late tonight and for a few nights while I try to catch up."

She swallowed her disappointment. She had

known that he had had to delay some of his jobs while his mother had been ill so he could stay with the girls. She hadn't thought about how that would play out as he tried to get back to a normal schedule.

She smiled anyway. "Then I'll make supper when the girls get hungry, and I'll keep your plate warm until you can be home."

Nodding his thanks, he folded his napkin and put it on the table.

He stood and started to pick up his plate to bring it to the table, but she waved him off. "I can handle the dishes. Mindy will help me. That way you can get back to us sooner."

She saw a brief glimpse of surprise and appreciation in his expression before he headed for the door. "Goodbye, girls—"

He was interrupted when Mindy burst into sobs and threw herself out of her chair and ran to him.

Surprise lit his face, and he swept her up into his arms. "Hey. What's all this?"

Mindy had been quiet as she had listened and watched the adults. She had been smiling not long ago. What had happened?

She sobbed noisily on David's shoulder as he gently rubbed her back, looking flummoxed. He looked to Ruby as if she might know what was going on. She had been able to guess that Mindy wanted that kiss to happen earlier purely because of the context. But she had no context for this. Where had Mindy's mind gone that she'd gotten so upset?

Mindy, who was *never* noisy, was sobbing loudly. One hand was fisted on her father's shoulder.

Ruby shook her head at David, as uncertain as he was.

From Ruby's arms, Maggie was watching her sister with her own bottom lip trembling. Ruby leaned in to touch her cheek to the toddler's. "It's all right, big girl."

David's eyes flashed as he watched Ruby, attention momentarily diverted from Mindy.

Ruby bounced Maggie gently. "Do you want to come into the living room and see if we can find something to play with?"

She took Maggie into the other room, where there was a wicker basket on the floor with blocks and two cloth dolls inside it. Maggie seemed happy to be set on the floor, and Ruby stacked blocks with her for a minute until she felt the girl was distracted enough.

She could hear David speaking to Mindy in the kitchen, and the girl's sobs had quieted. Ruby moved into the doorway, where she could still keep an eye on Maggie.

David sat on the chair pulled out from the table

with Mindy on his knee, and he was speaking calmly to the girl who watched his face with tears drying on her cheeks.

"You'll have a fun day with Miss Ruby. She isn't going to be working at the restaurant anymore."

Ruby felt a pang. Lovina had been right. She'd given her notice. And she'd lost her dearest friend because of her choices. Lovina had separated their schedules so they didn't see one another those last few days. Ruby would miss the activity and her regular customers, too.

She felt she was where she was supposed to be, but everything was different now. Maybe she would write Lovina a letter. Or invite her over for coffee soon. Try to apologize and make amends. Those were thoughts for another day.

Mindy had started to cry again, fat crocodile tears rolling down her cheeks. David looked up at Ruby, something helpless in his expression. She took a step into the room.

"I need your help today to get settled in," she told Mindy.

Maybe the girl hadn't understood and thought David was leaving her and Maggie alone?

David was clearly uncomfortable with the show of emotion and now stood up with Mindy in his arms. He brought her to Ruby, who held out her arms. Mindy reluctantly came to her.

"I saw one of your dolls in the living room. I can't wait for you to show me how to take care of her."

David asked her with a look whether she was okay and edged toward the door.

He had a lot of work to do and they both knew it.

Mindy burst into more noisy sobs as he moved toward the door. He looked back, and Ruby motioned for him to just keep going. "We'll be all right."

She could only hope it was true.

She hadn't expected Mindy to be devastated at her father leaving for the day. The girl had never had a problem when she and Maggie had been dropped off at Lily and Aaron's home.

But David had to leave, and there was nothing for it but to soldier on.

Ruby took Mindy into the living room, and Maggie promptly burst into tears on seeing her sister so upset.

It took Ruby several minutes to calm both girls down, and Mindy only stopped crying when Ruby asked to see the rabbit hutch outside. Ruby found herself with an arm full of rabbit.

She had thought she could handle the girls, but she had not been prepared for Mindy's breakdown. It set the tone for the whole day, with Mindy tearful and quiet. After Mindy's whispered words weeks ago, Ruby had grand dreams of having the girl talking by the end of their first week together. Obviously, she had given herself too much credit.

Maybe David's mother would have some insight. But by the time Maggie had lain down for a morning nap, Mindy had exhausted herself and fallen asleep on the couch.

Ruby retreated to the kitchen, where she slipped into one of the chairs and put her head in her hands.

Not for the first time, she wished her mother was still alive. *Mamm* had always seemed so knowledgeable about children. Ruby was having doubts whether she could be what the girls needed after all.

Chapter Twelve

"And they were friends from that day on." Ruby read the words from the last page of one of Mindy's books.

She was sitting on the edge of the little girl's bed. Mindy was tucked underneath the covers, crying again. Silent tears had been streaming down her face for the best part of a half hour.

Ruby and David had slipped into something of a routine these past twelve days. Things hadn't gotten better with Mindy.

And there was a part of Ruby that missed the man who'd paid her pointed attention, had courted her at the concert.

Earlier today, David had sent a message with a young neighbor boy that he had to help a customer on the far side of town, and he expected to be home late. So Ruby had gone about their day and was now putting the girls in bed.

Maggie was lying in her crib, drowsing in the low lamplight. Through the slats of her crib, Ruby could see her sucking her thumb, her eyes blinking slowly as she fought off the last moments of wakefulness.

Ruby reached out to smooth the fine hairs at Mindy's temple, curly because of the moisture from her tears. Mindy turned her head away, and Ruby let her hand drop to the quilted cover.

It was Friday now. Almost two weeks since that first morning together as a family, since Mindy had melted down in the kitchen.

Things hadn't improved.

Every morning when David left for work, Mindy started crying. She clearly didn't want him to leave. She'd tried holding onto his legs, tried blocking the doorway. This morning, she'd hit Ruby with her fist just after the man had walked out the door.

Ruby hadn't had a chance to tell David. She wasn't sure she was going to.

Several nights ago, she and David had stayed up late, trying to figure out a solution.

She watched David come home exhausted from working all day. His was a physical job. And then he'd come home and found the house a mess, with toys scattered throughout the living room and two little girls on the verge of tears. She didn't have a solution.

After that first day, Mindy had refused to be distracted by her bunny rabbits. Gone was the little girl who'd clung to Ruby, who'd drawn sweet pictures of them as a family.

Mindy threw tantrums when Ruby asked her to clean up her toys. She stomped her feet and fumed silently, and when Ruby patiently insisted that Mindy obey, Mindy cried.

Mindy also stuck to Ruby like glue. If Ruby left one room to go to another, Mindy followed. She wasn't eating like she had been before. She picked at her food and left much of it on her plate.

David was always so exhausted when he came home. He usually tucked the girls in, scarfed down the plate Ruby had left for him on the stove and closed himself into his bedroom. She assumed he went right to sleep.

Lying awake at night in her room down the hall, she found herself wondering if David would soon come to realize that marrying her was a big mistake.

She'd promised herself she was going to bring joy to his life. And she was failing.

They needed to talk. Things couldn't go on as they had been. Mindy was unhappy—more than that. From the way she gulped in sobs, unable to stop crying, her trembling…something deeper was going on. Ruby's arrival as part of the family had been some sort of catalyst, but not in the way she'd hoped.

Ruby didn't know what else to do. She reached out to soothe Mindy's shoulder, but the girl shifted away from the touch.

Ruby should've been more involved in the girls' nighttime routine. She didn't know how David tucked them in, what he said to them. Tonight might've gone more smoothly if Ruby knew what to do.

She started to hum a soft lullaby that she remembered her *mamm* singing to her as a little girl.

Mindy's eyes closed and she started keening, the soft cry startling Ruby into silence.

There was movement from the hallway, and David appeared in the doorway.

Mindy scrambled to get loose of the covers, and by the time she did, David was already there, kneeling beside the bed.

Mindy tucked herself into his embrace, and his arms came around her, cradling her close.

"Mindy *boppli*. What are you still doing awake?"

His words were said in a gently chiding voice that cut straight into Ruby. He couldn't know that she'd been sitting in this very room for an hour trying to calm Mindy, placate her, read to her so that she'd go to sleep.

She glanced toward the window, but since it was dark outside, all she saw was a reflection of the bedroom. David's dark head bent close over Mindy as he offered comfort.

Ruby's stomach knotted. She'd been so certain that she would step easily into the role of Mindy's mother figure. The girl had seemed to adore her before the wedding ceremony. She'd been compliant and sweet and easy to be around.

And now that Ruby was here in her house, she was none of those things. Her behavior had to be because of Ruby. And Ruby didn't know how to go forward from here.

She was tired. So tired.

Ruby turned from the window and the broken dream of being the one to offer Mindy comfort.

The girl's tears had subsided into snuffles, and now she yawned.

"Lie down," David said gently.

He helped Mindy back beneath the covers, smoothed the quilt over her little legs. He leaned in to kiss her cheek and *scritched* her cheek with his beard, earning a watery smile.

"It's time to sleep," he whispered. He glanced to Ruby, and she seemed to see the censure in his expression. She moved toward the door.

Mindy reached for him, clinging to his arm as he stood up.

"Mindy," he warned.

Ruby braced for her to start crying again, to make that terrible keening noise.

But her lips moved.

Ruby stopped short of the doorway.

David had frozen next to the bed. "What?"

This time, Mindy's whisper was audible. *"Daed."*

David dropped to his knees on the floor beside the bed. Ruby saw the rapid way he blinked. She knew how he'd longed to hear Mindy speak again, knew he must be experiencing such intense relief.

This wasn't a moment for her to intrude. She slipped out of the room and left the pair together.

When David came downstairs, Ruby stood in the living room beside the large window that looked out over the front yard. Her back was to him, but he could see that she was hugging herself, her arms around her middle.

The bottom step creaked beneath his weight, and she turned her head to acknowledge him, using one hand to wipe the tears from her cheek before she twisted away and hugged herself again.

The knot inside his gut tightened.

His stomach was rumbling with emptiness, and he had a headache from standing over the forge for most of the day, but he crossed the room toward her, stopping with the sofa still beneath them. He put his hands on its back.

"How long were you up there with her?"

She shook her head. Wiped her face again. "At least an hour. Maybe more."

An hour?

He'd stood unnoticed in the hallway for a few minutes listening to Ruby's story, watching through the cracked doorway while Mindy pushed her away. Ruby's feelings had to be hurt that Mindy was rebuffing her overtures, but she'd only shown kindness to his daughter.

"I thought things were getting better."

She hesitated. Then shook her head slightly.

Helplessness rose inside him, threatening to choke him.

After long days when he could finally focus on his work without worrying about his *mamm* or the girls, he'd finally felt as if he were catching up.

He'd come home in the evenings to find Mindy and Maggie overjoyed to see him. Ruby was pleasant as she'd provided his supper, and he'd fallen into bed happy and tired from a *goot* day.

What had Ruby gone through during the day while he'd been gone? More of Mindy's difficult behavior? And how could he help Mindy? He'd sat beside her bed upstairs waiting to hear her say something again. His name, anything.

She'd drifted off to sleep before he'd gotten his wish.

He felt inadequate. More so in the face of Ruby's tears.

"I'm s-sorry," she murmured, her voice wet. "I'm just tired."

Was she really apologizing for her tears?

He couldn't stand it anymore and crossed the last few steps between them to pull her into his arms. He told himself it was the same as holding Mindy. But that was a lie. Ruby fit *just so* in his arms. It was easy to rest his chin on the crown of her head. Her slender form tucked close was as different as holding a horseshoe versus a nail in the palm of his hand.

He could feel the heat of her breath where her face was pressed to his shoulder. She relaxed into his hold, and he found his heart beating in his throat.

"I didn't expect things to be perfect," she said. "But this has been more difficult than I thought."

He tensed, as much from how he was responding to holding her as to her words. He set her back gently.

"She should've been in bed much earlier."

She didn't say the words she easily could've: *You should've been home much earlier.*

Her shoulders sank. "I tried. She ran and hid downstairs. It took me twenty minutes to find her inside the bureau, and the entire time, I was terrified she'd gone outside and run away."

If he would've been here, maybe the whole situation could've been avoided. There still wasn't enough of him.

"Why didn't you ask *Mamm* and *Daed* for help?"

He knew it was the wrong thing to say even as the words emerged from his mouth.

"So your *mamm* can think I can't manage the girls?"

Mamm had lost track of Mindy before. She would understand. But he didn't say that, either.

He needed distance between them. If he let her get too close, his heart might get involved.

She turned so she was in profile to him. He could see her reflection in the window. Two more silver tears slipped down her cheeks.

He clenched his jaw against the urge to go to her. To hold her again.

She swiped her tears with the back of her hand. "I'm tired. I need to clean up in the kitchen, and then I'll go to bed."

She slipped past him into the kitchen. He stayed where he was and heard the rattle of dishes. Water ran. And then stopped. Soft sobs overtook the silence in the house.

He ran one hand down his face. He felt terrible. What could he do? He couldn't go to her. Couldn't hold her again.

This was why it was better to be like *Daed*. His *daed* kept everything inside. Never shared what he was feeling.

But the awful feeling twisting his gut didn't feel safe. It didn't feel good to listen to her tears, quiet as if she were trying to muffle them.

His stomach rumbled, reminding him that he hadn't eaten any dinner. But he couldn't go into the kitchen. Not now.

He went upstairs, got ready for bed. Sat on the edge of the bed. The door was open, though he didn't expect Ruby to walk through it. Was there anything left to be said between them?

He would talk to Mindy tomorrow. Make her understand that this behavior couldn't continue. He could ask *Mamm* to check on Ruby and the girls.

Ruby's soft tread passed by in the hallway. But she slipped past his doorway without stopping.

He turned off the battery-powered lamp and lay down. What could he do?

There was nothing good inside him, nothing to give Ruby.

Chapter Thirteen

Sunday afternoon, David was outside in the barn. Mindy had tagged along to check on the gelding, who should be healed enough to go back to work in another day or two.

They were petting the horse's nose when Ruby came searching for him with Maggie on her hip.

"There's someone looking for you," Ruby said. "A man knocked on the front door. An *Englisher.*"

Mindy immediately grabbed David's hand, sidling close to his leg.

Her behavior had improved since yesterday, but she still wasn't herself. She was petulant and frosty with Ruby. She'd clung to David all day yesterday and pouted through worship service this morning at the Glicks' house when she'd been forced to sit on the women's side of the room.

"I was thinking of visiting my father for a bit,"

Ruby said hesitantly. "If—if you wouldn't mind hitching the buggy for me. I can take the girls if you'd like."

Things had been strained between them since Friday night. The distance between them was his fault.

She was still weary. Heartsick. He could see it in the fine lines around her mouth and eyes.

Mindy squeezed his hand, her shoulder brushing against his leg.

"Mindy and I will stay." He didn't have it in him right now to talk her through a crying spell. "I'll hitch the buggy for you. Then after we talk to this *Englisher*, we'll clean out a few stalls, and then maybe walk over to see the Herschbergers' new kittens."

Mindy lit up with a smile.

Ruby didn't quite meet his gaze. She nodded.

Something inside him wanted to reach out and take her hand. Touch her elbow. Do something to break this fragile tension between them.

He didn't.

He hitched up the buggy and waved goodbye as she drove out of the yard.

David gave Mindy's hand a squeeze, and they traipsed across the yard toward the house. He rounded the house instead of going inside.

There was, indeed, an *Englisher* standing at the foot of the steps. He hadn't seen David and

Mindy come round the side of the house. The man twisted from the waist and looked back at the shiny silver sports car parked several yards away on the drive. He actually took a step toward the car before turning back to face the house. He ran one hand through his hair, muttering something David couldn't hear.

His actions made it seem as if he were nervous, and David couldn't help but wonder why. Who was he? David had never seen him before.

He had a remembrance of a few weeks ago when Ruby mentioned an *Englisher* had been looking for David in the restaurant. And Will had mentioned the same thing. But David had no idea who this was. Why was this man looking for him?

The man stood with his shoulders turned away from David, one hand now covering his mouth and jaw, staring at David's house. At the designs made out of horseshoes hung on the outside walls, maybe?

"Hello," David called out. Mindy was still at his side.

The man visibly startled. He spun and faced David fully.

The stranger now stared at him with wide eyes. David approached, Mindy still clinging to his hand, though her steps were dragging.

David was used to gawking *Englishers*. He'd

had several stop their cars on the side of the road to watch him work over the past weeks. He might be used to it, but he didn't like it. And whoever this was, his wide-eyed stare made the skin crawl between David's shoulder blades.

"I don't sell the art," he said. "Not anymore."

He'd done it as a hobby when Jessica had been alive. Made the designs at the forge in his free time. Sold some.

He stopped walking with several paces still between the *Englisher* and himself and Mindy.

The man had lost the surprised expression, now looking guarded. "I'm Todd. Barrett. Todd Barrett." He took two confident steps forward, the motion at odds with the way he stumbled over introducing himself. He stuck his hand out, and David reluctantly shook it.

There was something about him that David couldn't put his finger on. Maybe it was the set of Todd Barrett's eyes or the color of his hair— no hat to cover it—that made something niggle at the back of David's mind. He wore a fancy *Englisher* suit, though he was the same height as David. Some niggling thought, just out of reach, bothered him.

Todd Barrett's eyes tracked up and down David like he was examining him or something. It made David uncomfortable. He didn't like it, not knowing Mindy was standing right by his side.

"I don't sell the artwork," David said again. Hopefully that would be enough to get rid of the *Englisher*.

Todd followed David's glance over his shoulder and must've realized David was referring to the metal creations hanging from the front porch.

"Oh. But you—I mean, you're a blacksmith, right?"

"I'm a farrier." David said the words with more patience than he felt.

There was something about this interaction that was making him itchy. Todd was standing too close. He wasn't keeping his distance like *Englishers* usually did, and he kept looking at David like he was waiting for something.

"I wanted to—" Todd shook his head, cutting off his words. "I—"

Maybe he didn't know what a farrier was. "I shoe horses," David explained. "Do you have a horse?"

He had several *Englisher* clients who appreciated his work. Maybe one of them had made a referral, though they would've known better than to send someone to talk to him on a Sunday afternoon. Sundays were for rest and spending time with family.

"I was thinking of getting a horse," Todd said in a rush. It made David think he'd latched on to the idea right that moment. "Trying to get an idea of all the costs. You know."

David didn't know. He'd never thought about it before, but surely there had to be a better way of figuring out the costs of keeping a horse than this.

"Where's your property?" David asked.

"Oh, ah… I'm thinking of boarding it. The horse."

Wouldn't the boarding stable have a relationship with its own farrier? None of this was making sense.

Mindy tugged on David's hand and pointed at the fancy sports car.

Todd's gaze was drawn to her, and he stared at her as if he'd seen her for the first time, though he had to have noticed her when David had approached.

Todd swallowed hard, still staring, and David had had enough. He turned his body, and since Mindy was still clinging to his hand, she had no choice but to follow him so that she was half hidden from the stranger.

It didn't stop her from peeking around David's leg. She was scrutinizing Todd's face intensely.

"It's a day for being with family," David said, leaving no room for doubt that this was a dismissal. "If you want to talk business, you can find me during the week."

Todd swallowed hard again, his eyes tracking from David to Mindy. He opened his mouth, but nothing came out.

"*Goot* day," David said firmly. He gave Mindy's hand a tug, and they went up the porch, though it was more like he dragged her, because she was still staring at the *Englisher*.

David felt prickles down his spine for hours afterward. It was strange, indeed.

Ruby turned the buggy into Evan's driveway. She stopped the horse but let the reins go slack in her hands.

Could she even face going inside? She'd wanted a break from the breath-holding she'd been doing, waiting for Mindy to cry again. But now she was having second thoughts. She was almost certain Lily was going to take one look at her and realize something was wrong.

Ruby was unhappy. Wasn't she? She didn't know anymore. Maybe she should just go home.

Home.

David's house didn't feel like home.

Not when Ruby felt like she was tiptoeing around Mindy. The girl hadn't had a crying spell yesterday, but she had followed David around everywhere he went and had ignored Ruby on two occasions. David had corrected her, but when she'd complied with a petulant look on her face,

Ruby had known she wasn't really obeying in her heart.

Ruby glanced to Maggie, who was nodding off in her car seat.

She *did* want to see her father.

So she unbuckled Maggie, and the girl roused as Ruby walked up the front stoop to knock.

She was greeted at the door by Jacob with an enthusiastic hug. Apparently her brother Reuben and his wife Theresa were visiting this afternoon.

Jacob shouted to everyone else that Ruby was here, and soon enough, there was chaos. It wasn't peaceful, but having her family around soothed her.

She was plied with coffee and stories of everything that had happened during her two weeks away.

Her nephews' stories about school reminded her that she'd meant to prepare some space for Mindy in the house. She would join the schoolroom next school year, and Ruby's own mother had tutored her in her alphabet and numbers before that.

Even Jacob's too-loud voice didn't grate on her nerves the way it used to.

An affectionate longing rose inside her, and she realized she'd missed them.

Beth went to lie down for a bit, and Reuben was drowsing behind a book.

Maggie had fallen asleep on the couch, and Ruby made a pallet in one corner of the room and transferred the girl there.

She was washing up her coffee mug when *Daed* found her in the kitchen.

"Want to take a walk?"

"Of course." Spending time with him was why she'd come.

The afternoon had grown blustery, and Ruby was forced to brush wisps of hair out of her face. They walked together toward the grazing pasture.

"Is everything going all right?"

She nodded. Then shook her head.

He waited patiently while she sorted through her thoughts, just like always.

How could she say what she needed to without him thinking less of David? The man was doing his best, though she thought he was going a little too easy on Mindy. Babying her.

"I expected it would be easier to settle in."

"I wondered whether he would have trouble letting go of his wife." When Ruby questioned him with a gaze, *Daed* said, "I thought it might be difficult for him when you started arranging the house the way you like it."

Rearranging the house hadn't even crossed her mind. She hadn't even put out *Mamm's* quilt. She had been so concerned with what was going on with Mindy that she hadn't done any of that.

Maybe that was even part of the solution. If Ruby settled into the house, maybe Mindy would relax.

"When your mother and I married, she wanted to fix up everything just so." He shrugged. "I couldn't understand why it was so important to her. And she got frustrated with me when I asked why she was wasting her time with all of that." He smiled fondly at the memory, but Ruby was aghast.

"I've never heard this before."

"It's true. It took more than a year for us to really settle in together. I was stubborn, and…she was, too. We fought more than we should've."

Ruby shook her head, the thought of her mother and father arguing so foreign that she couldn't believe it. "You and *Mamm* never fought. You were her perfect match." She'd heard *Mamm* say so often.

"Not in the beginning. I'm not even sure she fell in love with me until after that first year."

He stopped walking to lean on the corral railing. She stood next to him, unable to relax. Unable to do anything but stare at him.

He didn't seem to be joking.

Neither did he smile and poke fun at her for believing him. He just waited for her to think this revelation through.

"*Mamm* never mentioned this before. Ever."

And Ruby had gone through a phase when she'd been ten when she wanted to know everything about how her parents had met and fallen in love.

"Maybe she was embarrassed. We both were, once we'd learned to communicate better. To compromise."

She'd believed her parents had gotten along perfectly, the way she remembered from her childhood. There'd never been an unkind word spoken from one to the other.

Daed seemed to know she was struggling. "It took me a long time to figure out what was really important. And how to make your mother happy."

"So you weren't a perfect match?"

"Nothing is perfect. We grew into each other. Grew into a deeper love, a more fulfilling relationship."

"*Mamm* told me you were a perfect match. And that I had a perfect match, too." It had been too painful for too long to talk about Jonathan, so she didn't say his name.

"Did she?" His faraway gaze was pinched with sadness.

"She was a good matchmaker. She paired up some of our friends."

"And several cousins. Reuben with Theresa and Aaron with Lily." Evan was younger. She'd never asked him if *Mamm* had matched him with Beth.

His lips twitched. "I don't know about that. Reuben was stubborn enough that he never would've spoken to a girl if he knew his *mamm* had picked her out for him. He and Theresa courted their own way."

Was that true?

She struggled to focus her memories, now fuzzy with age. Reuben had been married by the time Ruby was ten.

Had she rewritten memories, heard her mother wrong when she said that they were a perfect match? She felt as if the foundation she had built her hopes and dreams on had been shaken, maybe cracked.

"You'll figure things out with David. He's a good man."

"He loves his girls."

"I've noticed the way he looks at you," *Daed* said. "He cares for you. Probably just wrestling with himself because it happened so quickly after his wife died."

Ruby shook her head, her instinct to deny it. David had been kind enough and loaned her his strength Friday night when she had been so emotional.

She and David had agreed that this wasn't a love match. It was better not to have expectations like that.

The entire way home, she thought about what

Daed had said, about the way her image of her mother and father had realigned, the realization that they hadn't always been perfectly happy as she remembered from her childhood.

What did it mean? Had she been wrong all these years, thinking that her perfect match was lost?

Chapter Fourteen

David hadn't returned home feeling this despondent in a long time.

He took care of his horse and his tools and ensured the forge was properly cooled.

And he still remained in the barn, unable to face Ruby, Mindy and Maggie in the house, though he knew they were waiting on him.

Not yet.

When he'd arrived at his last call for the day, his friend Elijah had been waiting anxiously for him. His mare was foaling, and she seemed to be having a difficult time, and would David help? He'd soaped up his arm and put on one of the shoulder-length plastic gloves he'd learned to keep on hand and done his best.

It hadn't been enough.

The mare had lived, but the colt was gone.

Logically, David knew he'd done his best.

But he was heartbroken for his friend, who'd been waiting tirelessly for the prized colt. For the mama horse, who'd licked and licked her colt to no avail. David had had to turn away and wipe his eyes.

He didn't have the emotional energy to put on a happy face when he went inside. To deal with Mindy if she was being difficult.

But neither could he stay out here all night.

That was never more evident than when Ruby's soft footsteps carried her out into the barn. She stopped just inside the door, hesitating when she glimpsed his face.

"I… Mindy saw you drive past. She's been…" She shook her head slightly, cut off her words.

He could only imagine. Mindy was probably climbing the walls, waiting for him.

Ruby glanced around the perfectly clean barn. "Are you…are you coming inside?"

He nodded his head, but his feet didn't move.

The concern in her expression completely undid him, and he turned away, gripping the nearest stall door to stave off tears. His nostrils flared as he took a deep breath.

The rustling of her dress meant she was coming closer. "What happened?"

"I don't want to talk about it," he snapped. He realized he sounded just like his father the moment the words met his ears.

How many times during his youth had he left the barn reeling after hearing the same from his father? The old promise he'd made *not to be like Daed* burned his throat.

Everything inside him was tight as he turned, no idea what to say to make things right.

Ruby's face was pale, and her smile trembled. She was obviously near tears. "I'll just meet you back at the house, then."

She was gone before he could get his tongue untied or formulate any kind of apology. He just needed... If he could sleep, surely he'd be able to gather his thoughts in the morning.

He trudged to the house, not far behind Ruby. The lights shining from the windows in the near dark beckoned him. His bed beckoned him.

He kept himself together through saying a quick hello to the girls. He pleaded exhaustion and told Ruby he wasn't hungry when she offered him supper. They'd waited for him. The table was set for four.

Maggie was in her highchair, banging a small spoon against the table. *"Mamm!"* she shrieked. *"Mamm!"*

Had she—?

Had Maggie just spoken her first word?

Ruby looked over from the stove, where she was taking a pot off the heat. Her eyes were wide and guilty.

"Did she call you…?" He couldn't even say it.

"Mamm!" Maggie cried out happily.

But Ruby wasn't Maggie's *mamm*, and it should've been Jessica standing in the kitchen. The prickling behind David's eyes intensified. He couldn't catch a full breath.

Ruby was quiet as he excused himself. He stopped short in the living room.

Someone had moved the furniture all around.

"Did you—did you do this?" he called out to Ruby, voice hoarse.

She'd put Jessica's rocking chair right in front of the picture window, moved the two couches so they faced each other from the middle of the room. A crocheted afghan he didn't recognize was folded neatly across the back of the smaller sofa. And a small desk he'd never seen before was pushed against the wall near the rocking chair.

"It works better this way. Mindy will need space to learn her letters when we begin schooling here at home in a few more weeks. She should've started already, but…" Ruby's voice was subdued and became smaller and smaller as she spoke.

"You rearranged everything without asking me," he reiterated.

"We talked about this yesterday."

He remembered now. He'd been heading out

the door after breakfast, rushing while Mindy was distracted fetching a hairbrush from her room. Ruby had asked whether she could move a few things.

He hadn't expected her to change the entire room.

It was as if she'd erased Jessica's touch from the room entirely. He knew that his emotions were too raw from what he'd gone through earlier in the afternoon, knew he was being unreasonable.

"We'll talk about this tomorrow," he mumbled.

But when he turned toward the stairs, he realized the two small quilts Jessica had sewn were gone. They'd hung on the living room wall, artistic in their pattern and stitching.

Had Ruby moved them?

"Where are the quilts?" he demanded.

She shrank away from him, seeming small in the kitchen doorway. "Upstairs."

His mind was racing as he charged up the staircase.

Ruby followed him at a slower pace.

"You shouldn't have moved them. Jessica sewed those."

He looked over his shoulder on the landing to see her uncertainty from downstairs gone. Her chin jutted out at a stubborn angle. "This is meant to be my home, too, isn't it? That's what we agreed when we married."

"Things were fine as they were," he said stubbornly. He didn't even know his own mind, whether he meant the living room and the quilts or how things had been with him and the girls. His emotions were out of control. Like a limb that had fallen asleep and was now filling with painful prickles. Worse.

Ruby was taking Jessica's place, at least in Maggie's heart. She was preparing to teach Mindy her letters, the way Jessica would have if she had lived. Ruby wanted him to talk to her, but he *couldn't,* and it was all too much.

"I want the quilts put back." He tried to keep his voice even.

Now Ruby blinked back tears, clearly hurt. Guilt surged.

"Then you move them." She pointed into the girls' room and then turned and marched back downstairs.

A glance inside showed she hadn't put the quilts on a shelf or in a drawer. They were hung above each of the girls' beds.

This wasn't about her trying to hide Jessica's quilts after all. She'd moved them closer so the girls would see them every day. Sorrow swelled in his chest.

Maggie called out, *"Mamm!"* from downstairs.

He should apologize. He hadn't meant to lose his temper, to allow his grief to overwhelm him.

But the words remained pent up inside, and he closed himself in his room. Tomorrow. He'd do it tomorrow.

Ruby had hoped to clear the air between them, but someone knocked on the door before dawn, and David dressed in the dark and was gone.

The day wore on, and she didn't know whether she should move the living room furniture back to where it had been before.

It wouldn't change what was really wrong, and that was David wouldn't talk to her.

It couldn't be more obvious that he wanted Jessica, not Ruby.

And at some point, she'd started to care what he wanted.

By midafternoon, she had a terrible headache from the silent tears she'd shed last night and those that snuck up on her during the day—the ones she tried to hide from the girls.

She'd laid Maggie down for a nap and come back downstairs to put the pot roast she'd prepared in the oven for supper.

Mindy trailed her from room to room, silent and watchful. She'd been surprisingly quiet all day, not bursting into noisy tears like Ruby had thought when she'd told the girl David was already gone.

Ruby's tension headache felt like someone was

pounding a railroad spike behind her right eye. She couldn't go on like this.

She took Mindy into the living room with her. "I put some paper and crayons at your desk. Can you draw me a picture?"

Mindy's eyes narrowed. Ruby's patience frayed under the pain in her head.

"I'm going to lie down for a few minutes here on the couch. I need to rest my eyes."

Mindy shook her head.

"Mindy, my head hurts." Ruby sat down on the couch, wincing at just that movement.

The girl shook her head, this time more agitated. She came to Ruby's side and grabbed her hand. She tugged as if she wanted Ruby to stand up.

Ruby wanted to cry. Why couldn't the girl give her this? Fifteen minutes might take the edge off her terrible headache.

Ruby thought she heard a sound from the kitchen, an echo of the door opening, but she couldn't be sure with the way her head was pounding.

"Mindy, please." Ruby didn't want to fight. She covered Mindy's hand with her free hand and twisted the other so she was clasping Mindy's hand between hers.

"Just a few minutes. I'm only going to lie down—"

"No!" Mindy's voice rang out clear and terrified. A tear overflowed and ran down her cheek. "You c-can't sleep." Mindy's words wobbled. She kept pulling on Ruby's hand, almost sitting down in her fury. "Stand up."

Ruby tried to draw her close so she could hug her. "Mindy—"

"*Mamm* had a head-rake." Mindy was gasping the words now as tears streamed down her face. "And when she slept, she didn't wake up."

It took a moment for the meaning of the girl's words to hit.

Mindy let go of Ruby and slumped to the floor, burying her face in her hands. Near silent sobs shook her shoulders.

David had told her once that he worried Mindy had witnessed her mother slipping away.

Here was the proof from Mindy herself.

Ruby slipped off the couch and sat on the floor, whisking the girl into her lap. The pounding in her head hadn't receded, but she was so focused on Mindy that she barely felt it anymore.

She had tears in her own eyes for the pain Mindy had gone through as she pressed her cheek to the top of Mindy's head.

And through blurry eyes, that's when she saw David standing in the kitchen doorway, expression stricken.

He'd come home early. And it was obvious just

by looking at him that he'd heard what Mindy had just said.

"Don't s-sleep," Mindy said through her tears.

"I'm not. Not right now," Ruby whispered. She held David's gaze. Why wasn't he coming in here, coming to help comfort his daughter?

"I d-don't want you t-to die." Mindy's sobs shook her shoulders.

Ruby squeezed the girl gently. She tipped her head, inviting David to join them.

He hesitated but then stepped into the room. Just in time for Mindy to whisper, "I l-love you, Ruby."

The words filled an aching, empty spot that Ruby hadn't even known existed inside her heart. Tears slipped down her cheeks as David rounded the couch. His expression was carefully blank. She'd seen the way his eyes had widened and the hurt inside them when Maggie had called her *Mamm* in her baby voice.

David sat on the floor beside her. Mindy stirred at the motion.

"Mindy."

"Daed!"

Ruby saw the flash of love and surprise at Mindy's word. Saw the grief and sorrow hidden deeper behind it.

To her surprise, Mindy didn't scramble off her lap to go to him. The girl had wanted her father constantly every day but now only shifted in Ruby's lap so she could see him and reach out one arm toward him.

David clasped her small hand in his larger one. He seemed at a loss for what to say or do.

"Ruby's head hurts," Mindy hiccupped the words through her tears.

"I heard." His voice was rough, and compassion surged inside her for the man who'd been through so much.

He glanced at her, and from this close, he wouldn't miss her puffy cheeks and how the tip of her nose was red, like it always got when she cried.

His attention shifted to Mindy, and Ruby was grateful for that.

"Mindy, just because someone gets a headache, it doesn't mean they will die." It was clearly difficult for him to talk about this.

"B-but *Mamm* died." Mindy said the words with the simplicity that a small child saw things.

"She did. The doctor said…" David had to swallow hard.

And Ruby couldn't stop herself from reaching out to hold his hand.

He ducked his head for a moment. He didn't let go of her. "The doctor said there was something wrong inside her brain, and that's why she died. That's why she got a headache."

Mindy shuddered with a sob. "B-but, what if Ruby gets something wrong with her?"

David's gaze shifted to Ruby, and she saw the pain and joy in his eyes. He'd wanted Mindy to speak for so long...

But she was holding all of this inside, and it had to be painful for him to talk about it now.

"The doctor said that what happened to *Mamm* was a rare thing. It might not happen again to anyone you know in your whole life."

"Really? Not *Grossmammi*, either?"

"Is that what had you worried when she needed a nap?"

Mindy nodded, her head brushing against Ruby's shoulder.

"*Grossmammi* has something wrong with her heart. She's taking special medicine, and she's doing okay."

Mindy thought about that for long moments, then seemed to accept her father's reassurance.

There was obviously something still bothering the girl, because she shifted on Ruby's lap. She looked between her father and Ruby.

"Do you—do you think *Mamm* is mad that I love Ruby, too?"

She heard David's soft intake of breath. Mindy had spoken the question innocently, but it could still hurt.

His gaze snagged Ruby's. He glanced away, breaking the ethereal connection.

"No," he said, and there was a new hoarseness to his voice.

But he gently disengaged his hand from Ruby's.

Chapter Fifteen

Ruby's headache remained even after Mindy was settled with more hugs and reassurances. The girl kept talking, and David seemed shell-shocked to hear her voice.

He sent Ruby upstairs to rest. Her headache had come back with a vengeance, and she was appreciative for a break. She wanted to know why he'd come home early, but she couldn't think past the pain.

A short nap helped reduce Ruby's headache, though it wasn't totally gone when she woke. Afternoon light slanted through the windows, and Maggie was babbling softly from the girls' room, as if she'd just woken, too.

Ruby went in to change her, earning a happy gurgled *"Mamm!"* and a toothless smile.

I love you, Ruby.

Mindy's soft words from earlier played in her mind. It seemed surreal. All of a sudden, Mindy's behavior had come into clear focus.

When David left for the day, Mindy was reminded of the day he'd left and her mother had died. Everything had changed for her in that one day.

She was afraid of it happening again.

Knowing what Mindy's struggle was made Ruby feel as if she could help her. She didn't believe this was the end of Mindy's struggle, but at least she and David knew what it stemmed from.

At the landing, delightful scents of the roast she'd put in the oven earlier wafted up to Ruby and Maggie.

Downstairs, David and Mindy had set the table. In the center of the table was a little drawing Mindy must have worked on.

The girl ran to Ruby and wrapped her in a hug while David watched. There was something guarded about his expression, some emotion Ruby didn't recognize.

Later that night, after supper and dishes and reading and tucking the girls in, Ruby was tidying up the living room when David came downstairs.

"Is this one yours?" She held up the crayon drawing that had obviously *not* been done by a child's hand. The artist had drawn a near perfect picture of this house. It was shaded and neat and easily recognizable.

He scrunched up his face. "Yes. You can throw it away."

"Why?" Astonishment colored her voice. "It's amazing. I didn't know you were an artist."

"I'm not. I used to draw for fun when I was a boy, but… I stopped."

Why?

The question was on the tip of her tongue, but she held it back.

"We need to talk," he said quietly.

Her breath stuck in her chest. He'd been so careful to keep his emotion in check earlier when he'd been sitting close, talking with Mindy. Was he angry about what had happened? Upset?

"It's a nice evening," she choked out. The sun was just setting, streaking the sky with color. "Did you want to sit on the front porch?"

"Fine." He hesitated. "Do you…want some *kaffee*? Or something?"

She straightened, confused by the gruff tenderness in his words. If he was offering her *kaffee*, he couldn't be that upset. Could he?

"I don't need anything."

She'd never actually sat on either of the rocking chairs on the front porch. They were handcrafted and had been well cared for. There wasn't a splinter or crack to be seen. The chairs were slightly angled toward each other, and she had a clear view of David as he braced his elbows on his knees and put his head in his hands.

Her heart went out to him, but her throat closed

over whatever words she might say to offer comfort. He'd hurt her badly yesterday. Would he even want her comfort?

He didn't stay with his head bent, just rubbed his face and then straightened in his seat, both hands gripping the armrests.

"I'm sorry about yesterday." There was true remorse in his voice. "I was surprised when I saw that you'd changed things in the house, but I shouldn't have gotten angry. Shouldn't have raised my voice."

"I'm sorry, too," she said softly. "I should've asked you instead of just doing it. I'll put the living room back together if you want."

He shook his head. "This is your house, too. You can do—whatever you want."

The words were broken a bit, and she wished she was sitting as close as they'd been in the living room earlier. She would have reached out to him again.

"I don't want to erase her. Or replace her."

"I know."

"You…do?"

He glanced out into the dark fields beyond the yard. "Everything you feel is right there for everyone to see. It's no wonder the girls have come to love you."

She sat quietly for a moment. "I love them, too," she said when he didn't continue.

He still held himself back.

"You can trust me," she whispered.

He frowned. "Yesterday was…difficult."

She scooted to the edge of her chair. "Maybe it would help if you talked about it. I'm a *goot* listener."

"You don't want to hear what's in my head." He said the words like he really believed them.

"Yes, I do." She said it with all the earnestness she could muster. "We are in this together. We're friends." Of a sort.

He shook his head a little. She wished she could see his expression in the falling darkness.

And then a pair of headlights cut through the twilight, slowly heading up the street.

And then turning into the driveway.

David stood up, moving to the edge of the porch and putting one hand on the railing. He squinted into the darkness. Stiffened.

Did he recognize the sleek silver car? She didn't know what kind it was, but it was low to the ground and looked fast.

A man got out of the driver's seat. He killed the lights, and she saw tousled hair the same color as David's. He was built like David, too, as if they'd been cut from the same cloth.

He was clearly an *Englisher*, and she found herself puzzled and unable to look away from his face.

"Mr. Barrett, I'm not available to talk business tonight."

David knew the man? He must if he'd used his name. She knew he helped some *Englishers* with their horses, but there was some fine tension in David's shoulders that made her wonder what was going on.

"This isn't about horses." There was some resignation in his voice. Or hesitation. "It's important that we talk."

David glanced at Ruby. Back to Mr. Barrett. "This is my wife, Ruby."

Mr. Barrett nodded to her. "Todd Barrett."

She made an attempt at hospitality, though she wasn't sure David would want her to. "Can I get you a cup of *kaffee*?"

He shook his head. "No, thank you. I'll be up all night, anyway," he muttered.

David crossed his arms. She'd never seen him so standoffish. "What do you want?"

"I think you might be my brother."

The outlandish words echoed around the inside of David's head.

After Todd had blurted out the impossible, Ruby had seen David's skepticism and shock, so she'd taken over.

Like a seasoned schoolteacher, she'd started giving orders. Told Todd he better come in. She ushered them both into the living room. David sat on the rocking chair, while Todd sat on the couch, a leather briefcase beside him. She turned the lamps up, and the room felt blazing bright and also too small as she disappeared into the kitchen.

Ruby returned only moments later with two glasses of water. She handed one to Todd, and he thanked her with a smile.

David found himself scrutinizing every centimeter of the man's face. Was his smile the same one David occasionally saw in a mirror?

No.

All his fanciful, wishful thinking from his childhood couldn't have prepared him for this.

Ruby brought the other glass to David, and he thanked her with a glance. Or maybe she understood the terrified look in his eyes, because she stood at his side and put her hand on his shoulder.

"I know David's parents," she said. "He was born in this community."

"Actually—" David started.

"He was born in a Mount Vernon hospital," Todd said, interrupting him.

Ruby glanced down at David, her brows furrowed.

"My *mamm* lost two other babies. Doc Bradshaw considered her high risk and wanted her at the city hospital for my birth." David turned his stare on Todd. "But what does that have to do with—"

"Two miscarriages," Todd murmured to himself. "And two babies that died within eight weeks after they were born?"

David shook his head. "No."

But Todd was reaching into the leather satchel he'd sat beside him on the couch. He pulled out several pieces of paper. "I have copies of birth and death certificates here."

The skin of David's face felt too tight, stretched over his bones. What was Todd saying? That his mother had had two babies that had died?

"I'm sorry," Todd said. He held the pieces of paper in his hand but didn't try to press them on David. "I know this is a lot. I didn't know how to do this."

David shook his head. He still didn't understand.

"So what if my *mamm* had two babies that— that died?" He had to swallow hard on the words. *Oh, Mamm*. She must've been heartbroken.

"This is the death certificate for my little brother," Todd said gently. "You both have the same birthday. He died when he was four weeks old from a rare genetic disorder."

David was tongue-tied, but Ruby murmured, "I'm sorry."

He had never been so thankful to have her beside him.

"The same genetic disorder that caused the death of your siblings."

David still didn't understand.

"My mom and dad always thought it was a fluke…that Neil died. I have another younger brother, Henry. He's two years younger than you. Mom's been big into tracing her ancestry, and she convinced my dad to do one of those DNA tests. They can be used with ancestry websites to help you track down family you might not have known about…" Todd waved away the thought as if it wanted to take him on a wild-goose chase.

"That part isn't important. I'm finishing my residency, and I thought it would be interesting to look over Mom and Dad's DNA test results. But when I looked, neither of them had the genes that would cause them to have a baby with this genetic disorder." He tapped the paper still held in his hands. "Neither one of them," he repeated.

DNA tests, websites, family trees. What was he saying?

"I started wondering whether it could've been possible that Neil, my little brother, wasn't really my little brother. If somehow, he'd been switched at birth. At the hospital."

Instant denial sprang to David's lips, but he pressed them together. This couldn't be real.

Even if Todd was right, that there'd been some mix-up at the hospital, that didn't mean *David* was his biological brother.

"I hired a PI. A private investigator," he explained.

Confusion and shock crashed through David, and he wanted to toss Todd from his seat. He read. He enjoyed mystery novels. He knew what a PI was.

"I haven't told my parents, but…the guy I hired tracked down one of the nurses who'd worked on the labor and delivery floor the night you and Neil were born. She remembered that night. She told my PI that there was a bad storm. That part of the hospital had had electricity knocked out and a generator malfunction, and there'd been a lot of chaos. There was also one nurse working that night—who was later fired—who was negligent in her duties. The PI couldn't find any evidence that it was intentional, but it *is* possible that you were switched at birth with Neil. Is there anyone—your mom or dad, a relative—who could've done something like that?"

Daed. David didn't know why he thought of his father in that moment.

He stood up, Ruby's hand falling away. He went to the window and stared out into the darkness.

Something had unlocked inside him earlier in

the face of Mindy's grief. His emotions were out of control, refusing to be contained or ignored, the way he'd tried to do for so long.

He wanted to be alone. He needed to think.

Ruby's watchful gaze seemed to take everything in. She was here at his side.

We are in this together. We're friends. He didn't deserve her.

What Todd said seemed so unbelievable. It couldn't be possible…and yet. He'd felt something, some sense the first time he'd seen Todd. Tonight, he'd had a sense of foreboding seeing Todd get out of his car in the drive. Was this why?

There was silence in the room as David struggled to process everything that had been revealed.

His parents had lost two infants. They'd never told David about it.

Two babies born on David's birthday. One died of the same rare disorder David's infant siblings had.

A stormy night in the hospital. A negligent nurse.

A baby switch?

"Why come now?" David asked hoarsely, turning from the window. Now that he was finally figuring things out again after Jessica's death. Now that Mindy was talking again and needed him.

Ruby had sunk into the rocking chair and watched with concern.

Some private grief passed over Todd's expression but quickly cleared away. "My father—our father—had a health scare late last year. I need to know before it's too late."

David shook his head. "There's no way to know if anything you said is true."

"There's one way. If the two of us submit a DNA test, it could tell us if we are brothers or not related at all."

David's heart thudded in his ears. If it was true, did he want to know it?

What if it wasn't? What if Todd Barrett had it all wrong?

He was David Weiss. Son of Amos and Leah. Not a Barrett. Not an *Englisher*.

But Todd might stir up trouble if he spread rumors around. David's *mamm* didn't need any more stress added to her heart.

"What do I have to do?"

Chapter Sixteen

"Is that a kitten?"

David's affectionate grumble made Ruby look up from the noodles she was readying to add to a pot of boiling water.

She'd seen him drive his work wagon to the barn and knew he would be coming inside any minute.

She still wasn't prepared for the way her breath caught and her heart pounded in her throat.

"Very observant," she teased. "Did you also notice she has ears and a tail?"

The kitten in question was sleeping in a long, flat wicker basket tucked in the far corner of the kitchen. She was a calico, a colorful patchwork of orange and black with only a few splashes of white.

She was tiny, barely six weeks old.

"Daed!" Mindy shouted from the living room,

where she'd been playing with Maggie while Ruby kept one watchful eye on both of them.

Mindy ran into the room, skirts flying behind her. "Didja see my new kitty? Isn't she cute? She's a *goot* girl. She even drank some milk from a saucer!"

David squatted to greet his daughter, and Ruby saw the vulnerability and gratefulness on his face as she chattered about the kitten. It was gone by the time he stood up.

It hit Ruby hard, how much she had come to care for him. She was grateful for the excuse of stirring the pasta sauce on the stove and turned away from the father and daughter.

From the corner of her eye, she saw Maggie toddle into the room. Her face was lit with excitement, too, and she made a beeline toward her *daed*.

"Dada!" she shrieked, because Maggie only had one volume, and that was at the top of her lungs.

"What?" David roared playfully. He broke away from Mindy momentarily to go to Maggie and scoop her off the floor. "What did you say?"

"Dada!" Maggie squealed happily, patting his bearded cheek.

"She said *Daed*," Mindy added, singularly unimpressed.

Probably because she'd heard Maggie chanting the word all afternoon as Ruby had practiced and practiced with her.

Ruby put down her wooden spoon. When she looked at David, he couldn't hide the joy shining from his expression. He was staring at her wonderingly. And behind all of that, there was a question in his expression. One she didn't know how to answer.

So she teased him instead. "It's what we named the kitten."

He gave a rumbly growl and came after her, Maggie still in his arms. It was Ruby's turn to shriek, and she twisted away just before he grabbed her, darting across the room.

It was so unexpected, and Maggie chortled from his arms, and Mindy giggled and clapped as Ruby evaded him, but she didn't move very fast, and it didn't last long.

Cornered between the table and chairs. David's fingers tugged the back of her apron.

She turned to face him, and the action put them face to face. She was breathing hard from the exertion of running around the kitchen, and his eyes sparked at her when they scanned her face. Today she hadn't had time to check on her appearance. She probably had flyaway wisps of hair coming out of her prayer *kapp*.

"You've got…" He let go of her apron, his arm falling away from what had been *this close* to an embrace. He lifted his hand to brush something from the corner of her mouth. "Spaghetti sauce," he explained. But his hand lingered, cupping her jaw even after the sauce she'd tasted earlier was gone. Something shifted in his eyes.

She was caught in the magnetism of his gaze, breathless.

But Maggie shrieked, *"Daed!"* from far too close a distance.

Ruby winced.

David's hand fell away, the openness in his expression gone.

He glanced to the side, and she followed his gaze to see Mindy squatting near the sleeping kitten, watching it.

"Do you want to tell me *why* there's a kitten in the house?" he murmured as he took a step back.

She could hear the water on the stove bubbling, and there was a sudden hiss. She moved to the stove more quickly than she'd evaded David, and she saw his raised eyebrow.

Maybe she had wanted to be caught, she admitted to herself as she turned down the burner and stirred the pasta to keep it from boiling completely over.

"Mindy has her rabbits, and when Maggie gets older, she'll probably have a guinea pig or goat or a trained bird or even an alligator. I thought it was only fair that I have a pet of my own."

"And when your cat decides to terrorize Mindy's rabbits or eat Maggie's hypothetical bird?"

Ruby affected a haughty look. "*Daed* is a responsible kitten. She would *never.*"

Mindy jumped up from her squat, but the kitten didn't wake. "Do ya wanna see her ball of yarn?" She scampered into the living room without waiting for David's answer.

"We are *not* naming her *Daed,*" he complained plaintively.

Ruby couldn't control the smile that was twitching at her lips, and he pulled a face at her. "Very funny."

Mindy raced back into the room, skidding a bit on the floor in her sock feet. She held aloft a small ball of red yarn, already hopelessly tangled by the kitten's play earlier.

But David's stare remained on Ruby, who felt a slow flush creeping up her cheeks.

"Why are ya lookin' at Ruby like that?"

That was enough to break his stare.

Mindy glanced between the two adults. "Do ya think she's pretty?"

A blush burst into Ruby's face like an inferno.

David's eyes snapped back to her.

She wished Mindy wouldn't have put him on the spot like that. He didn't—

"Ruby is very beautiful."

There was no room for doubt in the steady, serious way he spoke.

Ruby's heart pounded, sending blood rushing into her ears. David thought she was beautiful?

"More beautiful than Betty?" Mindy asked.

Betty was the mare David had borrowed from his friend.

One corner of David's mouth kicked up. "More beautiful than Betty."

"More beautiful than a tulip?"

There was some history behind why she'd asked about a tulip. There had to be. Maybe it was her favorite flower.

"More beautiful than a tulip."

"What about a whole batch of tulips?"

"More beautiful than that."

David's eyes danced, and Ruby found she couldn't look away, even though the sauce needed stirring. He really thought she was beautiful.

Pleasure infused her, warming her from the inside out.

Mindy cocked her head, her gaze a little too cunning when she turned it on Ruby. "Do ya think *Daed* is beautiful?"

Ruby heard David's sputter even as she had to hide a smile behind her hand. She quickly put on a serious expression, not wanting to hurt Mindy's feelings.

"Handsome," she told the girl. "Your *daed* is handsome."

Mindy's eyes narrowed. "More handsome than a prince?"

David took two steps and scooped Mindy into his arm from behind. Now he had both girls.

"Oh, no. We're not repeating all that. Let's go wash up for supper."

He carried the giggling girls out of the kitchen, but not before Ruby saw the hint of redness above his beard.

David—stoic, serious David—was blushing.

David walked beside Ruby in the backyard. Mindy had begged to play outside after supper, and the cool, pleasant evening was perfect for it.

Mindy was pulling Maggie across the yard in a small red wagon.

"Do you think she'll fall off?" Concern filled Ruby's voice.

The wagon was bobbling over the uneven turf. Maggie was holding on to one side, weaving back and forth thanks to Mindy's erratic driving.

"Probably. But she's not far from the ground, and Mindy isn't going very fast. She'll be all right."

She sent him a sideways glance. "If you're sure."

He wasn't sure about anything. He didn't know what had come over him tonight.

Maggie had said *daed*, and Mindy had been chattering, and his heart had been so *full*.

His feelings had bubbled over like boiling water from a pot.

Your daed *is handsome*.

He'd blushed like a schoolboy at Ruby's sincere compliment.

Since the afternoon Mindy had spoken—the night Todd had shown up out of the blue—things had changed between him and Ruby. It was as if something had broken inside him, releasing his emotions from the stranglehold he'd had on them.

They wouldn't be bottled up again.

When Ruby was uncertain about something, she turned toward him instead of away.

He caught himself watching her. Often. More often than he should. Noticing things about her, like the kinds of foods she enjoyed and those she ate because it was expected. Wondering where her mind went when she stared off into the distance.

He'd almost reached for her hand last night. The girls had been asleep, and he and Ruby had ended up on the couch together, both reading. It had seemed the most natural thing in the world to reach for her hand, to want to share affection with her. His hand had even twitched before he'd quelled the thought.

What was he thinking? It felt dangerous for his heart to become entangled again.

He'd shut himself off after Jessica's death to protect himself from experiencing pain.

He'd begun to treasure the tentative friendship he and Ruby had struck. But didn't that mean he could be hurt all over again? He knew Ruby had wanted a perfect match. And he was pretty sure he wasn't it.

And he didn't even know who he was. What if…what if Todd was right?

He'd always longed for a sibling. Always felt there was a part of himself missing. He vividly remembered a time when he'd been about Mindy's age, asking his *daed* why he couldn't have a brother and *Daed* telling him never to speak of it again.

What if he had two brothers out there somewhere?

He'd been trying to put Todd's outlandish story out of his mind. It couldn't be true.

But…

What if it was?

Had his father known? Had his father done it? Stolen some other family's baby so that he and *Mamm* could have a baby of their own?

He thought of his reserved father, the man who had taught him right from wrong, had helped him with arithmetic problems during his school days. The man who'd had tears in his eyes when he'd first held Mindy as a *boppli*.

David didn't think his father could do something like switch a sick baby for a healthy baby. But he'd also seen people who made terrible decisions when they were mired in grief.

Now David felt Ruby tense up beside him, and his gaze fell on the gelding happily wandering out of the barn.

Ruby took one sidestep toward David.

"It's all right." He clicked his tongue at the horse.

Mindy dropped the wagon tongue and ran toward the horse. "Horsey!"

Ruby inhaled sharply beside him. He stepped to intercept Mindy, putting a hand to her shoulder. He spoke to the horse, and the gelding slowed to a stop. The horse lowered its head for Mindy to rub its nose, then it whickered.

"How did he get out?" There was definitely a hint of worry in Ruby's voice.

"He let himself out. For the second time. When I got home yesterday evening, he was loose in the barn. He must've figured out how to open the latch on that stall I've got him in."

She didn't look impressed like David had been.

"He must be sick of being cooped up. Wants to go back to work. He doesn't have a mean bone in his body," David said. "He won't hurt her."

David glanced at Ruby. "Or you. Maybe it's

time you made peace with your fear. You never know when you might need to hitch him up."

She looked at David with wide eyes. He wasn't going to push her. If she didn't want anything to do with the horse, he would let her be.

"Do you trust me?"

Maybe he would never be her perfect match, but he could give her this. Help her overcome this fear, even if just a little bit.

Her expressive eyes landed on him, and he saw the resolution in them when she made the decision.

"Come here," he said softly.

She hesitated for a split second and then came to stand at his side.

He ran his hand down the horse's neck. The gelding was perfectly still.

"He won't hurt you. I won't let him." Not that he thought the horse would anyway. "Do you want to try?"

Mindy had been distracted by a butterfly she was now chasing across the yard, and Maggie was gurgling happily from the wagon.

David looked over at Ruby. She was backlit by the setting sun, which turned her skin golden.

She looked hesitant, but there was also an edge of curiosity to her expression. She nodded slowly.

David's left hand still rested on the gelding's neck.

He held out his right hand to Ruby. Had he

been looking for some way to touch her, since he hadn't last night? He couldn't say for sure.

She slipped her hand into his, and he guided it to a place close to where his other palm rested on the horse.

Beside him, Ruby took one shaky breath. When she inhaled the next time, she was steadier.

"Nothing to worry about. Not with this guy."

David could let her go now. He *should* let her go.

But he didn't.

Chapter Seventeen

The letter arrived while David was gone for work.

Ruby was weeding the flower beds against the front porch when the postman came up the walk.

Mindy was pushing Maggie in the baby swing tied to a low branch of the sycamore in one corner of the front yard. She called out a greeting, and the postman waved at her.

Ruby smiled at him, thinking what a difference a few weeks had made for Mindy.

And then she took the bundle of letters from the postman, not realizing how grubby her hands were until she streaked dirt on the envelope on top.

It was from the DNA test company. It looked terribly official, with its crisp white envelope and fancy square typeface.

Ruby slipped the entire bundle of letters in

her apron pocket, suddenly anxious. What would David do when he arrived home and she gave it to him?

She knelt beside the flower bed again, but her thoughts wandered, and instead of weeding, she found herself sitting back on her heels and idly watching the girls.

She was…happy here. With David and the girls.

Mindy had cried a bit when David had left for work yesterday morning. But it wasn't the sobbing tantrum she'd thrown before. A few tears had fallen, but she'd allowed Ruby to hug and comfort her. A few minutes later, she'd been distracted by her doll, and the day had gone on. Ruby loved listening to her chatter. The girl could talk about anything.

Maggie seemed to want to follow in her sister's talkative footsteps. She had surprised them all by saying *dog* and *horse* when they'd been in the yard two nights ago.

Ruby's feelings about David were more complicated. She was always aware when he entered a room. Missed him while he was gone during the day. His touch made her heart pound, and she craved seeing his smile.

She was falling in love with him. She had come into this marriage believing it was impossible. They both had.

She hadn't told him. She'd kept these feelings, which were new and too overwhelming, to herself. She didn't want to change things between them, to make things awkward. He was still grieving for Jessica. And he was grappling with what Todd Barrett's visit meant.

And now the test results were here.

Later that night, she nursed a cup of tea at the kitchen table as David finished tucking the girls in for the night. The kitten slept in her basket in the corner.

David had left the stack of letters—with the DNA test results right on top—out on the counter. She'd given it to him as soon as he'd stepped in the door earlier, but he'd put it aside and focused on his family for the evening.

Would he open it now?

She heard his steps on the stairs and stood to go to the *kaffee* pot. She poured him a cup and met him at the table.

He wore a peculiar expression on his face. "You know how I like my *kaffee*?"

"Oh." Her cheeks heated. "A dab of milk, right? Or did I mess it up?"

"No, you didn't mess it up." He looked like maybe he wanted to say something more, but he only shook his head slightly. "I suppose I should open the results. At least I can put Todd's questions to rest."

So, he didn't think it was true? He'd never said as much out loud, and she'd wondered.

"Do you want me to stay?" Her stomach flipped as she waited for him to answer.

He nodded and relief flooded her.

She sat back down at the table with her coffee cup while he brought the letter to the table. He sat his mug on the table and took the chair next to hers. Their knees bumped beneath the table as he sat down beside her.

He opened the envelope with deft fingers.

And then he laid it on the table. Picked up his mug and took a sip. Put the mug back down. "I don't know if I can do this." She was so used to him keeping his feelings to himself that when he said the words so matter-of-factly it took a moment for them to register.

He met her gaze with a wry half-embarrassed smile. "It's silly. I already know it won't be a match. But I'm nervous."

"Do you want me to read it first?"

"Would you?" He slid the letter across the table to her, and she picked it up. There wasn't much in the envelope. It was light. She took the piece of paper out.

There was a soft squeak from the floor as David's foot jiggled up and down.

Distracted, she reached out and put her hand

on his knee. She hadn't even realized she'd done it until his hand closed around hers.

He was obviously more nervous than he let on.

But she didn't let go of him as she scanned the letter held in her opposite hand.

Oh, David.

"You are a DNA match with Todd Barrett," she said softly. "Enough of a match to be a sibling."

His grip on her hand grew crushing as she turned the letter toward him and pushed it across the table so he could see. His head bent, and his lips moved slightly as his eyes scanned the page.

Both of their mugs forgotten, he stared across the table at nothing. Had he forgotten she was there, too?

He started to raise both his hands and seemed to remember he was holding on to her. Tightly.

"Sorry," he muttered and let her go.

She tucked her hands on her lap, and he pressed the heels of both hands into his eye sockets. He shook his head, dropped his hands. Looked at the letter again.

"This can't be real," he said faintly.

What did it mean for their family? That David was born to *Englisher* parents, that he had two *Englisher* brothers?

And what about Amos and Leah? She'd seen how much they loved their son. They'd devoted their lives to raising him. They doted on their granddaughters.

She thought about the miscarriages he'd mentioned and the death certificates for two tiny babies that Todd had brought with him as proof.

His parents would be devastated to find out that David wasn't biologically theirs after all this time.

All of this and more must be running through David's mind right now. He sat silent, brooding.

She wished he would talk to her. To let her in. What was he thinking?

She reached out and put her hand on his shoulder. It startled him, and he blinked, as if only now realizing she was still here beside him.

He didn't reach out, didn't touch her this time. He stood up.

"I need to call Todd. It's early enough. I can walk over to the Herschbergers' barn." Their friends and neighbors had a telephone in the barn and didn't mind if other Amish families needed to borrow it.

His gaze went across the room to where the staircase would be if he could see through the wall. "The girls—"

"Of course they shouldn't be alone. I'll stay." Her heart was in her throat. He could go next door and ask his mother to stay with them.

If he wanted Ruby with him.

But he only nodded. A muscle ticked in his jaw. He opened his mouth to say something but then changed his mind.

He went out into the night.

David wanted to scream as he walked down the dark driveway and turned up the street.

His world was disintegrating around him. He'd seen the veiled hurt in Ruby's luminous eyes just before he'd tore out of the house.

But he couldn't stay and talk to her. How could he explain what he was feeling when he didn't even know himself?

He wasn't a Weiss. He'd passed on his name to his girls without knowing it wasn't really his. Given his name to Ruby when he'd had no right to do so.

He stumbled in the dark because he wasn't paying enough attention to see where he was going in the low light.

That's how he felt right now. Stumbling through the dark with no end in sight.

Was he a Barrett? He might've been born one, but he didn't know either of his biological parents. What were they like? And there was another brother, Todd had said. Younger than David.

He had brothers. Two brothers to fill the empty void in his heart that had always wanted a sibling to play with, share secrets with, partner with.

How different would his life have been if he'd grown up with two brothers? He wouldn't have felt so alone.

He barely knew Todd. What was his other brother like?

He turned around. He couldn't call Todd tonight, not with so much turmoil rioting through him. He didn't even know what he would say. What did Todd want from him?

He would have to let Todd know about the results another time. Soon.

But right now there was only one thought in his mind. He had to find out whether his *daed* had known.

He bypassed the house, knowing Ruby was inside. Was she waiting up for him?

He steeled himself and kept going, hesitating in front of his parents' house. The lights were off.

What would *Mamm* think?

His *mamm* had been the one to comfort him when he'd gotten scraped up climbing to the hayloft in the barn. She'd listened to him when the first girl he'd admired had said something unkind about him and his feelings had been bruised. She'd taught him how to make cookies simply because he'd asked.

He didn't want to hurt her, even though he *had* to confront *Daed*.

He went to the barn first. *Daed* often worked

late. And he guessed right, because there was a light on inside.

Daed glanced up when David entered the barn. He looked the same as ever, his face lined and tanned, same blue shirt. Same suspenders.

He nodded a hello and went back to planing a board on his workbench.

David couldn't help himself from staring, trying to find one thing that made them alike. Maybe the test had been wrong.

For the first time, he noticed the age spots on *Daed's* hands, new lines around his eyes. He looked older than David remembered.

It was quiet in the workshop, only the rhythmic sound of *Daed's* planer against the wood. David struggled for words. Couldn't find any. Hurt and anger swirled inside him. After a long time, *Daed* looked up.

"Everything all right?"

"No," David said hoarsely.

Daed reached for his planer again, and David erupted.

"Can you please put that down for a minute?" *Pay attention to me. I'm drowning here.*

Daed kept his eyes focused on the planer in front of him.

"You're not my *daed*," David blurted.

Had he meant to hurt his father with the way he'd blurted out the statement? He didn't know.

Daed dropped the planer. He bent to retrieve it.

David had never seen him lose focus or drop a tool like that. He didn't look at David when he straightened. Didn't say anything, but he also didn't start using the tool again.

"It's true." David still couldn't believe it. "I took a DNA test. I'm not your biological son. Someone switched me with another baby in the hospital the night I was born."

Did you know?

Did you do it?

The words remained trapped in his chest, screaming only from the inside.

"How do you know this?"

"A man came to see me. His name is Todd Barrett."

No reaction from *Daed* at the name. But his father was a master at hiding his emotions.

David felt fragile, his emotions too much on display.

"He had a copy of two birth certificates with your name on them. And two death certificates for the same babies."

Daed shook his head, eyes now bright with unshed tears. "I don't want to talk about that."

And all the chaos inside David tumbled loose. "You *never* want to talk about it. When I would bring up why I didn't have siblings, you never answered me."

Daed now put the planer to the wood as if his motions with the tool could drown out David's words.

"I needed to know," David said, his voice getting louder. "I would've understood why you didn't want me to bring it up if you just would've *told me*."

Daed kept planing. Was he even listening?

"Is this why you never wanted to talk to me?" David asked, the words torn from him. "Because I'm not really your son?"

Now *Daed* looked up, his planer going still. "You are my son."

"No, I'm not." David's temper rose. "Did you know it the entire time? Did you switch your son for me—a healthy baby?"

"That's enough." *Daed* wore no expression. David had seen him closed off enough times before. He wasn't going to talk.

David had always walked away before, knowing it was hopeless and that he'd never get what he wanted from his father.

But not tonight.

"Did you know?" David yelled. "I have to know! I have a right to know!"

Daed turned away, moving to a workbench that faced the opposite direction. He picked up a chisel and small hammer.

David waited, his pulse buzzing angrily in his ears.

He hated the man standing not fifteen feet away. He'd taken David from his true family and given him nothing.

He was still giving David nothing.

He wanted to scream. *Daed* wasn't going to give him the information he wanted.

Maybe he never would.

Still seething, David turned away. He was almost at the door when his father said quietly, "If your *mamm* finds out, this will break her heart."

Her heart.

David slipped out of the workshop into the cooling evening air. Ruby had told him that his mother had had a fainting spell just yesterday. She had a doctor's appointment this coming week and had insisted she was fine, just stood up a little too fast. But what if it was more than that? What if the medication wasn't working anymore?

And what if *Daed* was right? What if David told her everything he knew on a quest for answers, and her heart failed?

He would never forgive himself.

Knowing he was still too upset to go inside and face Ruby, he paced in the darkness between their two homes.

He was out of control. Shouting at his *daed* like he was ten years old again. He wasn't shut off from his emotions anymore. Not since that day with Mindy. Now he felt everything.

Including feelings for Ruby that were growing too big. He'd loved Jessica with all his heart, and it had broken him when he lost her.

If he let his feelings for Ruby grow, he risked being broken all over again.

He couldn't do it.

Their marriage was supposed to be a match of convenience. His feelings weren't supposed to be a part of it.

He needed to find a way to keep his distance.

Chapter Eighteen

The farmers market arrived Saturday, and it certainly felt strange for Ruby to be on the opposite side of the table from Lovina.

The autumn sun was shining, and the leaves had finally turned. Ruby had a warm sweater wrapped around her shoulders. The girls were happy as magpies, riding in a red wagon that Ruby pulled.

But David wasn't happy.

David had put his walls back up. She didn't know what had happened after he'd gone to phone Todd Barrett—because when David had come inside, he'd muttered, "I don't want to talk about it," and gone to bed.

Two days had passed, and she felt the difference between them keenly. Whatever openness had been between them was gone. He'd shut off the part of himself that had chased her around the kitchen and gently encouraged her to pet his horse.

They'd wandered around the periphery of the farmers market until Ruby knew she couldn't avoid the restaurant's booth anymore—where Lovina would likely be.

David motioned her on when one of his friends hailed him and claimed to need to talk about his horse's hooves.

And there was Lovina, her cheeks pink from the cool breeze. She stood alone in the booth as a couple moved away, purchases in hand.

Ruby's stomach quivered at seeing her former friend. They hadn't spoken in weeks. But it would be rude not to go over and say hi.

Lovina hesitated behind the table that separated the booth from the main walkway. She looked as if she might turn away and give Ruby the cold shoulder.

But Ruby walked up to the table anyway. "Hello, Lovina."

"Hello."

"I… I just wanted to say I'm sorry about the way we left things."

"I'm sorry, too," Lovina said. "I was jealous, I suppose. We'd been friends for so long, and it felt like we'd both be spinsters forever. And then David and the girls came along…"

"Mamm!" Maggie shrieked, interrupting Lovina's words.

Mindy tugged on Ruby's apron. "Can I have a cinn'min roll?" she whispered loudly.

Lovina raised her eyebrows while Ruby pulled out some money to pay for one of the decadent rolls.

"Share with your sister," Ruby told Mindy, putting the cinnamon roll on its plate in between them on the wagon. She would have to take them to wash up later. Hopefully that would distract the girls for a few moments.

"And I abandoned you like all the other waitresses," Ruby whispered. "I'm sorry."

Lovina shook her head. "I was afraid of losing your friendship. So I pushed you away."

"We'll always be friends. Come over and visit soon. Please?"

Lovina nodded, her expression warm and settled. "It seems like things are going well for you. Are you happy?"

Ruby glanced over her shoulder to where David stood several yards away still talking to his friend. Just looking at him swelled up her emotions.

When she turned back to Lovina, tears pricked her eyes. Lovina reached across the table to squeeze Ruby's hand.

"I… I think I'm falling in love with him. And he's still grieving his wife."

Lovina let her have a minute to just breathe and hold off the threatening tears.

Then she said, "Just because he lost someone doesn't mean there won't ever be room in his heart for you."

The words were completely unexpected. Lovina had always kept her tragedy to herself, so this seemed out of character.

Until Ruby caught her friend's quick glance over Ruby's shoulder. She turned her head to see the candlemaker in his booth. He was watching them. He smiled broadly and waved.

When Ruby turned back to Lovina, her friend was blushing. And smiling.

"Lovina…?"

"It's completely new, and I don't know if it will go anywhere."

"How? What?" Ruby didn't even know what to ask.

"He saw me in the booth alone a few weeks ago." After Ruby had resigned. "And he came to check on me. Helped me unload a few crates. And we…started talking."

"I can't believe it."

Lovina's eyes shone. "Neither could I. I'd held on to a broken heart for far too long."

Ruby glanced down to see Maggie smearing

icing all over the wagon. She pulled a face at Lovina. "I want to hear all about it. Will you come for a visit soon?"

Lovina nodded. "I will. And don't give up on your David."

Ruby glanced backward to find David watching her, even though his friend was still talking to him. He wasn't smiling, but his stare had a peculiar intensity that made her stomach do a slow flip.

She'd thought…she didn't know what to think, not after David had put his walls back up.

"Grossmammi!" Mindy's exclamation pulled Ruby's attention from her husband. Amos and Leah were approaching through the crowd.

Leah wore a smile for her granddaughter, who was waving excitedly.

David must've seen them, too. His expression tightened and he excused himself, coming toward his parents.

Amos looked tense, almost fearful. What had caused that?

David ignored him and moved to hug his mother, his expression almost sad.

Ruby's gaze lit on an *Englisher* family standing not far away. All of them were staring at David.

Ruby's breath caught as she realized one of the men was Todd Barrett. What was he doing here?

He stood next to another man, a few years younger, who had similar features to both Todd and David with slightly darker hair. An older couple stood slightly behind them. Tears rolled down the woman's cheeks.

Was this David's family? It had to be. But what were they doing here? Had David invited them?

All of those questions and more rolled around inside her head like marbles spilled on the floor. None of them staying still, just bouncing around.

David must've sensed something was wrong because he followed her gaze. His body went rigid.

She saw the way his jaw tensed, knew he must be battered by surprise and uncertainty. Her heart went out to him.

The woman who must be David's biological mother stared at his face with an expression of mixed hope and disbelief. She mouthed a name. Not David's name. She started toward David, and Todd put a hand out to stop her.

David threw a panicked glance in Ruby's direction, and when his eyes darted to Amos and Leah, she guessed that he didn't want them to know what was going on. Or maybe he was worried for his mother's health.

"Why don't you come this way?" she said to Leah. She wracked her brain, quickly coming up with a solution. "The girls and I could use some refreshment. What about you, Leah?"

Ruby lifted Maggie from the wagon and put her hand on Mindy's shoulder, ready to make a quick getaway.

Amos must've seen the Barrett family, because his face looked like a thundercloud, and red appeared on his cheeks above the dark line of his beard. "She's right. Let's get a lemonade."

But Leah didn't follow Ruby as she stepped away.

Mindy held back, too, dragging against Ruby's hold. "Who's that with *Daed*?"

David had taken a tentative step toward the Barrett family, as if he wasn't sure he wanted to meet them.

Leah still hadn't moved. Her voice trembled as she asked, "Who are those people?"

David heard *Mamm's* softly voiced question behind him. He couldn't find it in himself to turn and speak to her or even to ask Ruby to take her away.

He'd seen the understanding pass across her expressive face when he couldn't utter the words. Or maybe he'd just wanted to see it so badly he'd imagined it.

His pulse beat loud and hard in his ears, muffling everything else. What was Todd doing here?

David was tongue-tied, and his hands went clammy as the full realization of who was standing in front of him settled. These were his biological parents. His brother Henry.

David's eyes didn't know where to land and finally darted to Todd, who looked nervous. He wore jeans and a brown sweater and had two days' worth of stubble on his chin.

"What are you doing here?" David was vacillating between panic, frustration, anxiety and something else he couldn't even name. His rioting emotions made his question snap.

He hadn't called Todd.

He'd spent the last two days since his confrontation with his father trying to figure out what to do next.

He wasn't ready for this. Wasn't ready to see these people he was supposed to belong to but had never met before.

"I got a copy of the results." Todd's voice was rough with emotion. "I tried to get them to wait, but..." He shook his head with a smile that invited David to commiserate. As if David was supposed to know what came after the *but*. But they wouldn't listen? But they didn't believe the results?

Maybe David would've known the answer if he had grown up a part of this family.

But he hadn't.

"These are…my parents." Todd stumbled over the introduction. "Michael and Kimberly."

"Please call me Mom," the older woman whispered.

David shook his head wordlessly.

Everything felt like it was spiraling out of control.

The man beside her with salt-and-pepper hair stared at David with his mouth half open. He was clean-shaven, and David could see a muscle ticking in his jaw. The same one David could feel ticking in his own jaw.

David didn't know them, didn't know what he was supposed to feel at this moment. Happy? Was he grieving for the lost years? He was so confused.

"This is Henry," Todd introduced David's younger brother. That was enough to shake David out of this place of unfocused thoughts in his brain. He had always wanted a little brother.

Sounds that had been muffled all around him suddenly sounded perfectly clear.

"Who are those people?" He heard his *mamm* repeat her question.

"David needs to talk to you, but this is not the place to have that discussion." Ruby seemed to be the only one who had her head on straight. He wanted to hug her.

Meeting the Barretts like long-lost family out

here in the farmers market where all his neighbors and friends would overhear was not ideal. Did he even want to talk to them? He was overwhelmed and sad and suddenly so, so tired. He just wanted all of it to go away.

He looked back to catch Ruby's steady gaze. Everything he was feeling was mirrored in her eyes. She knew him, though he hadn't meant to let her in. Even though he'd pushed her away.

She had Maggie on her hip and one hand on Mindy's shoulder. He heard the soft gasp from Kimberly Barrett behind him.

"You have...daughters?" She sounded teary.

He couldn't look away from his *mamm*, who looked frighteningly pale. Ruby noticed, too, and let go of Mindy to reach out and put her hand under *Mamm's* arm. "Sit down."

His mother's eyes closed for a moment, and everything tightened up inside him. For a few seconds, he thought she was fainting.

He looked back at the Barrett family and the hope in Kimberly's face and the familiar concern on his father's expression. He held a hand out as if to ward them off. "I need some time. My *mamm* needs me."

He heard Kimberly gasp behind him, heard Todd's murmur to her.

He couldn't focus on any of that right now. He had to go to his *mamm*.

Someone at the nearest booth, selling honey and candles, saw his mother threatening to faint and pulled the chair out from behind his booth for her.

David went to her, conscious of footsteps from one of the Barretts behind him. Why wouldn't they just go?

When he turned to tell whoever had followed him to go away, Todd was right there. "I'm a doctor, remember? Let me help."

Todd directed his next question to *Mamm*. "Has anything like this happened before?"

Daed looked stricken. He couldn't answer. And *Mamm* was so pale David wasn't sure she could speak. So he did. "Yes. She has a heart condition." To Ruby, he said, "Can you take the girls away?"

"Of course."

When he thought she'd just leave, she reached out and threaded her arm around him. She hugged him tightly and then left, disappearing into the crowd.

She'd offered him comfort. After everything. He didn't deserve her.

Chapter Nineteen

David didn't usually fire up his forge this late in the day. He didn't usually stoke the fire so hot.

But today he needed the motion of swinging his hammer over his shoulder. After reeling in the shock of seeing his biological parents for the first time, after watching his *mamm* struggling for breath, he needed to hit something. Better to strike a horseshoe than do damage to his workshop.

The air around him had chilled as the evening wore on, but he barely felt it as the heat and sparks from the forge floated upwards.

He'd been out here all afternoon and evening after Todd had helped settle *Mamm* in bed and given further instructions.

Mamm had been pale and weak, but she'd insisted in a barely there voice that she was fine.

She wasn't fine.

He wanted to blame the Barretts for showing up unannounced in such a public place. If *Mamm* wouldn't have seen them, she might not have had this spell.

But if he was placing blame, shouldn't he take the brunt of it?

He'd had two days to tell *Mamm* about the DNA test. He could've walked across the yard and told her. She would've still been blindsided, just as he was. How could she not be?

Daed should've been the one to tell her. But of course he hadn't. *Daed* never let anyone in.

David struck the horseshoe so hard that he lost his grip with the tongs, and it flew from the anvil, striking him in the thigh before flying into the dust and hay several feet away.

Wonderbarr.

"Are you all right?"

Ruby's soft question startled him. He set his palm against the throbbing place on his thigh. He didn't want her out here.

"No, I'm not all right." Before she could say anything, he added, "And I don't want to talk about it."

He saw the flash of hurt move across her face. It intensified the chaos inside him.

"You should be asleep."

There was a small stubborn lift of her chin. "So should you."

Night had fallen over an hour ago, but his thoughts were nowhere near close to being able to settle for the night.

"I brought you something to eat. You haven't had anything since breakfast." For the first time, he noticed the cloth-covered plate in her hands.

"Just leave it." He hadn't been able to touch his lunch, not with the way Mindy had stared at him across the table with wide-eyed uncertainty. He'd come out to the workshop not long after that.

"No."

He was already bent over reaching for the horseshoe, but now his gaze snapped back to her. *No?*

"You'll feel better if you talk this out."

"Don't you mean you'll feel better?" he snapped.

"I'm not the one out here clanking loud enough to keep all the neighbors awake."

His nostrils flared. He picked up the still-hot horseshoe in his gloved hand and wiped off the hay and dirt stuck to it. He'd struck it so hard that it was misformed on one end.

He would have to start all over.

He tossed it on the ground next to the anvil, where it landed in the dust with a thud.

"What do you want me to say?"

"Anything."

Anything was too dangerous.

"How can I tell you what I'm thinking when I don't even know myself?" His volume rose dangerously.

"Just tell me that."

"When I saw the Barretts… I don't know. I can't even explain what was going on inside me."

"So, you didn't invite them?"

"No! I hadn't even called Todd yet to tell him the results. Apparently he got a copy in the mail."

David was still reeling from how quickly it had all happened.

"You look like your brothers," she said quietly.

He shook his head. What was he supposed to say to that? He had barely had time to glance at his younger brother.

"I don't know if I want to look like them. I've spent twenty-eight years thinking I was an only child. What am I supposed to do with two *Englisher* brothers?"

He'd always wanted siblings. But not like this. Todd and Henry were strangers.

He felt pulled in two different directions, even though he hadn't spoken to the Barretts long enough to know what they wanted from him. Todd had hinted at having a relationship. But David didn't know what that looked like.

"I don't know who I'm supposed to be anymore," he muttered.

He was Amish. He'd dedicated himself to the

Amish church at age seventeen. What was he supposed to do with all the expectations from both sides?

"And *Mamm*—"

"Todd said your *mamm* is going to be fine."

It would be a long time before David could erase the memory of her pale face and the sickly sweat that had beaded her upper lip.

He didn't want to think about that anymore, didn't want to think about talking to *Mamm*. She had asked him to talk to her, to explain what was going on.

She'd been deathly ill, but she'd worried about *him*.

He'd put her off. Told her that she needed to rest. She'd insisted he come over first thing tomorrow morning, or she'd chase him down.

She was stubborn enough to do it, even to the detriment of her health.

But he didn't want to do it.

What if she had a bad reaction when he told her he wasn't her real son? What if he shocked her into having another episode? What if it was worse? What if she didn't recover?

When Jessica had died, he'd understood why some people died of a broken heart. He didn't want that to happen to *Mamm*.

And he'd had the girls to think about. Knowing that they needed him had kept him going, forced him to get out of bed each day.

If he told his mother that he wasn't really her son, what would she have to live for? He couldn't forget about the two tiny caskets and two babies who had never been born.

He realized he had been lost in his thoughts, staring off into the distance. Now he refocused on Ruby, who was standing there with his plate of food in her hands. She'd stayed up well past when she should have been asleep. The girls were early risers, and she would lose sleep because of him.

And yet she was still there, concern in her expression, concern he wasn't sure he deserved.

It was too much.

"I don't want to talk anymore," he said before she could argue with him. "I don't have anything else to say."

He saw the faint tremble of her lips before she firmed them. She didn't smile, didn't argue with him, just put the plate on the nearest sawhorse and walked back toward the house.

He hated this. Hated hurting her.

He couldn't go on pretending. He didn't know who he was. He wasn't an *Englisher*. But was he really Amish? How could he be Ruby's match, be what she needed, when he didn't know his own identity?

* * *

Ruby hadn't slept a wink last night. She'd heard David come in sometime after she'd been in bed. It could've been minutes or hours after he had dismissed her from his work area outside.

He had gone down the hall to his bedroom. Had he spent a sleepless night like she had?

This morning, he was nowhere to be found, and she couldn't sit in the house worrying, not without upsetting Mindy, who was already watchful and quieter than usual. She intuitively knew something was going on.

Ruby made the impromptu decision to go see her *daed*.

She braved the barn and managed to hitch the buggy by herself. Only because David had shown her that his horse was gentle. Mindy chattered the entire time.

Ruby considered turning around as they passed the Bensons' farm, which marked the halfway point to Evan's home. Why should she burden *Daed* with her hurt feelings?

But Mindy would be disappointed if they turned back.

They arrived at Evan's before Ruby had decided what she should say. Maybe nothing.

Lily answered the door. Her hands were wet. "Beth has been having awful nausea in the mornings. I came over to help her with laundry day." Lily seemed to take one look at her and her mouth pursed.

Not goot.

"Jacob, take the girls upstairs to play."

The older boy groaned even as Mindy and Hannah raced up the wooden staircase.

"Be quiet!" Lily called after them. "Do you want a cup of *kaffee*?"

"Is *Daed* here? I need to talk to him."

Lily shook her head. "He and Aaron went out to patch some fence in the north pasture. I'm not sure how long they'll be."

Should she just take the girls and leave? It might make for awkwardness next time the family got together.

She reluctantly followed Lily into the kitchen. And was surprised when Lily poured her a cup of *kaffee* and then went into the utility room behind the kitchen. Ruby sat at the table in the corner nook and could see Lily scrubbing something in the big sink next to the washing machine.

The peacefulness lasted all of a minute before Lily gripped the edge of the sink and spoke, her voice carrying through the doorway so Ruby could hear it.

"Aaron said I pushed too hard—before you were married, when I asked you to move in with us. I wanted to say I'm sorry."

What was this about? Ruby's mind couldn't seem to catch up. "I don't understand."

Lily looked over, a wry smile on her lips. "I was a lot younger than my two older sisters."

Ruby knew there were several brothers in Lily's family and that she was the youngest.

"I always wanted to spend time with the two of them, and they never wanted me around. Too many years between us. When I married Aaron, I…" She shrugged a little and looked down into the sink. "I saw a chance to have the sisters I'd always wanted. Aaron told me more than once that I was trying too hard."

Was that the reason she'd share gossip? Why she was always in Evan and Ruby's business? Less so with Beth, but Beth and Evan had only been married for two years.

"I didn't know that," Ruby said quietly.

Lily must've thought that having Ruby live in their house would make them grow closer. How surprising.

"We've been married eight years, and sometimes I still feel out of place."

Compassion stirred, and Ruby wanted to give her sister-in-law a hug, but she stayed at the table.

Lily's hands splashed back into the water. "It's silly. Aaron understands me. He always has."

Ruby's stomach pinched. Here was another reminder that Aaron and Lily were a perfect match. And she and David weren't.

Lily shook her head. "I don't know why I want something more. I'm very happy." She turned a smile on Ruby, one that looked genuine.

And Ruby still felt that deeper compassion, as if she understood Lily a little better. "You are an excellent knitter, and I've always wanted to learn. Maybe you could...teach me?"

Lily's face lit up. "*Ja?* You'd...you'd want me to?"

"*Ja.* We're sisters, after all."

Lily went back to her washing, now with a small smile on her lips.

Ruby felt restless, happy that she and Lily had had this moment but still with unresolved feelings about David. She moved to stand at the window with her *kaffee*, listening to Lily tell a story about the muddy footprints Jacob had tracked inside yesterday, until she saw her father walking up from the fields toward the barn.

She quickly put down her cup and excused herself.

He saw her coming before her feet hit the bottom porch step. Called out when she got close. "What a *goot* surprise!"

She burst into tears before she had even reached him.

He didn't hesitate to pull her into his arms. "What is the matter?"

She was too worked up to answer. She just shook her head and more tears came.

When her crying had subsided some, she eased back from his hug. He pressed a handkerchief into her hand and let her go.

"All right. Tell me what's got my Ruby girl so upset."

"I thought things were getting better with David. It seemed as if he was opening up to me more. But now—" Now he'd pushed her away. "I don't think he trusts me at all."

She said the words, and they weren't quite right. They didn't settle with her. It was almost as if David didn't trust *himself*.

I don't know who I'm supposed to be anymore.

"Did I make a mistake when I married him? Maybe I shouldn't have tried to settle for someone who isn't my perfect match."

Daed didn't answer right away. He examined her face, looked out across the field dotted with cows. "Why do you want perfect? Can you achieve perfection?"

She shook her head.

"*Mamm* wasn't perfect. And I sure wasn't, either."

He'd told her that once, but she hadn't taken it to heart. *Mamm* and *Daed* had been married for twenty years before she'd died.

Ruby waited for him to say more. Obviously

he'd decided that his marriage wasn't a mistake, though he'd told her they had fought a lot in those early years. Her parents had been happy. They had shared everything with each other.

Did I make a mistake?

No.

No, she didn't believe she had. She'd gone into this marriage with her eyes open. She had known from the start that David wasn't going to fall in love with her. When had she expected his feelings to change just because hers had? That wasn't a fair expectation.

Wait a minute. Her feelings had changed?

She thought about the girls. Maggie's joy shone through whenever Ruby entered the room to get her after naptime. She said *Mamm* when she wanted Ruby. It wasn't just a word she was babbling. There was intention behind it.

And Mindy... Ruby thought about the Mindy who had been so silent and watchful when she had first met her. The girl who had been so desperately afraid of Ruby falling asleep and never waking up, who was finally starting to settle and believe that her life could be *goot* again.

Last night, while she and Ruby had been reading a book together on the bed, Mindy had leaned close to see the pages. She was already picking out letters after only a few lessons.

Mindy had looked up at Ruby with pride in

her expression, and Ruby's heart had swelled with love.

Ruby wouldn't trade her relationship as the girls' mother for anything.

"I don't know what to do," she whispered to her father.

"Don't give up on him. He needs you, probably more than he can say."

She wasn't so sure about that. David seemed determined to handle things on his own, especially his feelings. He'd let her in once but then pushed her away again.

It was her choice now.

And she wasn't going to give up on David. She didn't know whether he would ever be able to love her, but she was going to keep loving him.

Chapter Twenty

David stood on the back stoop of his parents' home with one hand resting against the door and his head leaning against his forearm.

He didn't think he could do this. He was about to break his mother's heart.

And he couldn't stop thinking about the way Ruby's eyes had darkened with hurt last night when he'd told her he didn't want to talk to her.

There came a gentle knock through the door.

"Are you going to stay out there all morning?"

It was *Mamm's* voice, and she sounded as hale as when she'd been ten years younger. Her words both made him smile and brought tears to his eyes.

He took a deep breath and opened the door. His father was there, nursing a cup of *kaffee* at the kitchen table when normally he would be in the workshop.

"*Kaffee* is made, if you want some," his *mamm* said.

She was doing dishes, and he had to bite back the words to ask his *daed* why he wasn't up and doing them. He knew *Mamm* was stubborn. She was doing the dishes because she wanted to.

"Let's hear all of it." *Mamm's* words left no room for arguing. David glanced at his father, whose gaze was turned down to the table.

"Don't you want to head out to your workshop? Since we're going to be *talking.*"

The words were aimed at his father, and they were childish. David felt slightly abashed when his mother sent him a look from the sink.

"Don't disrespect your father."

David swallowed hard.

Daed hadn't even looked up.

Whatever *Mamm* had said to make him stay inside must've been something.

"I think you had better sit down for this," David said to his *mamm*. "Are you feeling all right?"

She waved off his concern, though she did put the dish towel on the counter and turned to him.

"I missed my morning pill yesterday. That's what caused the spell while we were at the farmers market. Whatever you have to say isn't going to upset me."

"Don't be so sure," David said. "I still think you better sit down."

She came and sat between them. She took David's hand on the table and laid her other hand on his *daed's* forearm.

How many times had they sat like this? With *Mamm* always between them, always the one connecting them?

David swallowed the old hurt and cleared his throat. He wished he had gotten a cup of coffee, just for something to do with his hands. "What do you remember about the night I was born? In the Mount Vernon hospital?"

Her gaze went far off. "I remember the moment the nurse put you in my arms. How beautiful you were. How bright-eyed."

David shook his head. This was going to break her heart.

"There was a mix-up at the hospital on the night I was born. Apparently there was some chaos and a negligent nurse. I—I was switched with another baby in the nursery."

He saw her confusion. He made himself just say the words. "I'm not your biological son."

He barely choked out the words. *Mamm* squeezed his hand, and for a moment, he wished Ruby was here. She would've put her hand on his shoulder, would've offered a comforting touch.

But he'd gone for a long walk this morning,

and by the time he had come home, she and the girls were gone.

Now his mother looked puzzled. "How can you know such a thing?"

He told her all of it. About Todd finding him, about the private investigator, about the DNA test.

She came to the conclusion on her own.

"So those people at the farmers market were your biological parents."

"And my brothers." Emotion filled up his throat saying the word. *Brothers.*

He wanted to know Todd and Henry, he realized.

Mamm had tears in her eyes. "And the baby? What happened to the *boppli* that was supposed to come home with us?"

David's insides twisted painfully. "They loved him. He died when he was almost a month old."

He dug into his pocket for a handkerchief, offering it to *Mamm* at the same time that *Daed* offered one with his other hand.

David scowled, but *Daed* wasn't looking at him.

Mamm took the handkerchief from *Daed* and dabbed at the tears rolling down her cheeks.

David watched her closely. Her cheeks were still pink, and she was breathing normally. She seemed okay.

But he hadn't shared his suspicions about *Daed* knowing about the switch. Yet.

Maybe he didn't have to. He tried to take his own feelings out of it. So what if *Daed* had known? If the fact that David wasn't his biological son was the reason he'd never talked to David, never shared his heart, things weren't going to change now.

Daed wasn't going to suddenly start loving him just because *Mamm* knew the truth. So, maybe he should just keep his suspicions to himself.

His jaw locked, and he forced his gaze out the window. The bright sunlight felt a little off in the wake of the sad news he'd had to deliver.

"You don't seem surprised," *Mamm* said, and David's gaze was drawn back to her. She was looking at *Daed*, and David realized she'd meant the words for him. "I suppose you and David already talked about this."

A crack of bitter laughter escaped David. *Daed* talk?

But *Mamm* sent him a quelling glance.

Daed looked sorrowful.

Mamm waited. And waited. Long past the moment when David's impatience grew. Longer.

When *Daed* spoke, his voice was hoarse. "I suspected. When you were a babe, after we'd been home from the hospital about two weeks."

Mamm didn't gasp with outrage, didn't berate him. She was a better person than David.

"This is why you didn't love me." The words came from between clenched teeth as David fought through the pain.

Daed's head finally came up, confusion written on his features. "What?"

He shouldn't have said anything. But everything that had happened during the past weeks had put a crack in the wall he'd kept his emotions behind—and he couldn't seem to seal it up again, no matter how hard he tried.

"You didn't love me because I wasn't your real son." It made sense now. David could see it. "That's why you never wanted to have deep conversations with me, why you always pushed me away."

Daed shook his head even as *Mamm* murmured, "Oh, David."

"You are my son," *Daed* said fiercely. "How could you think I don't love you?"

David burst up from the table. "How could I think it? You proved it. Every time I came to talk to you, and you kept your advice to yourself. You never talked to me. Never shared yourself."

He was breathing hard, like he'd run miles under a hot summer sun. He'd never dared to say any of this before. But there was also some part of him that was relieved to have it out in the open.

Mamm was looking between *Daed* and David, concern written on her face. "Your *daed* has always been a man of deep emotions. He feels things deeply, though he doesn't always speak of them."

David felt his shoulders hitch. Shook his head slightly.

Daed rubbed a hand down his face. In that moment, he looked much older than his age. He stared at the table. "I—I didn't know. Not until later. It was terrible, waiting those few weeks. Thinking you were going to…" *Die. Daed* swallowed hard.

Underneath all his pent-up anger, David's compassion stirred. It was obviously difficult for *Daed* to talk about this. If it wouldn't have been so important, if he hadn't waited so long, maybe David would have let him off the hook.

But he needed to know.

Daed still stared at his hands on the table. "After that first month passed, then the second, and you were healthy… I suspected that maybe something happened at the hospital. Maybe the doctor had done something to you… Or maybe we'd been given someone else's baby."

Mamm inhaled audibly. *Daed's* head tilted toward her, but he couldn't quite meet her stare.

"I suspected, but how could I know? I'm not a doctor. Not a…an ancestry specialist. And by that time, we loved you—" His voice broke.

David's breath caught in his chest. How many times had he yearned to hear *Daed* say he loved him?

Daed cleared his throat. "I didn't ask questions because I didn't want to do anything that might cause us to lose you. You were our son."

But he hadn't been. Not really.

And because his *daed* hadn't gone back to the hospital, David had grown up without knowing his two brothers. Without knowing Michael and Kimberly. He'd always felt like a part of him was missing. Always ached for siblings to play with, to share his life with.

But neither could he blame his *daed*. Not after learning about two miscarriages and two tiny babies dying. His father hadn't switched the babies. He didn't really know what had happened. All he knew was he had a healthy baby boy. David could understand that, though everything happening like this made him ache with an unsolvable grief.

"If I held myself back from you—it was only because I feared losing you." Finally, *Daed* looked at David. "I didn't realize how deeply I'd hurt you. I'm sorry."

David looked at him and saw a man who'd lost so much. And been frightened of losing more. He could see *Daed's* sorrow, his regret.

And it finally loosened the bonds of David's

hurt and anger enough that his compassion filled him and overtook them both.

"*Daed*, I love you, too."

Maybe it had been what they both needed to hear, because *Daed* buried his head in his hands, crying softly.

David went to him, hugged him. *Mamm* stayed in her chair but put a hand on both of their shoulders.

David finally understood why his father had kept himself separate. It was a way of protecting his heart. But it had hurt David, and it had hurt *Daed*, too.

Was that kind of hurt what he wanted for Ruby? He'd pushed her away to protect himself from being hurt again, but he was doing the same thing *Daed* had done. How could he expect different results?

He couldn't.

And he didn't want that for Ruby.

He loved her.

The realization crashed over him like a mighty wave.

She'd come into his life to help his daughters. He hadn't been prepared for how knowing her, how receiving her care would change him.

She was everything.

But would she forgive him for pushing her away?

Chapter Twenty-One

Since Ruby and the girls were gone, David worked out in the shop with his *daed* for nearly an hour.

With everything that had been unspoken between them aired out, he felt different. Gone was the tension and hurt feelings he'd carried for so long.

He heard the buggy coming up the drive before he saw it. His heart leaped at the thought of seeing Ruby.

Daed seemed to sense it and gave him a knowing wink. "Maybe you could help me with this cabinet another time." In the rough words was an invitation, one that David was happy to accept.

"Count on it."

David crossed the yard, waving to Ruby as she pulled in close to the barn.

He went to help her out of the buggy.

"Look!" He could hear her speaking to the

girls even through the door. "*Daed* came to say hello to you."

He smiled and greeted the girls, but his eyes came right back to Ruby. He couldn't read her expression, thought maybe it was wariness in her gaze.

He wanted to blurt out everything. His conversation with his *daed*. His feelings for her. But he hesitated, knowing that Mindy was a little pitcher with big ears and not sure he wanted to say all he needed to say in front of her.

He handed Ruby out of the buggy, and she reached back in for the girls as he moved to unhitch the horse. Was it naptime yet?

All of a sudden, he noticed a car was pulling into the drive. It wasn't Todd's flashy sports car, but he saw his brother in the driver's seat. Another man was beside him. Henry? And two others in the back seat. It must be his parents.

Ruby saw them too and moved to stand next to David with Maggie in her arms. "I know it's been difficult for you to talk about what's going on," she said quickly. "I know you're doing your best, and I am grateful for everything you've been able to share with me. Last night, I couldn't stop thinking about what you said out by the forge. About not knowing who you are supposed to be." She looked at him with earnest eyes. "I know who you are, David. You've shown me.

It's there in everything you do. You're a loving father. A devoted husband.

"Your faith is unwavering. You are a man that people can count on. Your parents, your friends, even strangers. *Englisher* or Amish, you'll still be the David that I—that I care about."

She stumbled over her last words. Had she been going to say something else? He wished for a longer time to talk to her, wanted to hold her close and say everything that was in his heart.

But Todd was getting out of the driver's seat of the car.

Ruby reached down for Mindy's hand. "Come on, girls. Let's go find a snack and play inside."

He snagged Ruby's arm before she could walk away. She looked at him, surprise etched in her expression.

"Please, will you stay? I need you to stay with me." The words were easier to say than he had thought.

Her surprise turned into resolution. "Of course."

Todd approached slowly, hands in his trouser pockets. No one else had gotten out of the car. "Maybe we shouldn't have come. Mom and Dad promised they'd stay in the car. But we couldn't call, and we wanted to find out how your mother is doing."

It put David at ease that he still called *Mamm* David's mother. "She seems like her normal self."

Todd nodded. "My parents are really sorry about how everything happened at the farmers market. I'm sorry that I didn't warn you we were coming. They'd really like to see you—just to talk for a few minutes. But they told me to tell you that they would understand if you're not ready for that."

With Ruby's hand clasped in his and her shoulder brushing against his arm, David felt ready for anything. "We could probably put some *kaffee* on, don't you think?" He directed his question to Ruby, who smiled gently.

"I've even got some cinnamon buns left from breakfast yesterday."

Todd looked relieved.

He went back to the sedan as David and Ruby took the girls inside. David settled Mindy at her little desk with a small chalkboard and some chalk, and Maggie on the floor with her blocks. He went into the kitchen to see if Ruby needed help.

"Are you nervous?" She shook her head. "Don't answer that."

"You can ask anything you like." He took some mugs out of the cabinet and put them on the kitchen table.

She seemed surprised and pleased at his words.

"I am nervous." He went on. "I don't know what to expect."

A few moments later, there was a soft knock on the front door, and David grabbed Ruby's hand when she would've stayed back in the kitchen.

They welcomed the Barrett family into the living room.

Henry looked around curiously, while Kimberly stared at the girls, and Michael couldn't seem to look away from David.

"I don't know what to say." Michael spoke first.

David let out a shaky breath. "I'm glad it isn't only me."

His mother's eyes raised to him, and he saw the tears sparkling there again. "I can't believe it's really you. We want to know everything. We've missed so much."

He chuckled. "Everything is a lot. Why don't we start with the basics? This is my wife, Ruby."

Introductions were made, and his *Englisher* family settled in, taking seats around the room. Ruby was personable and full of smiles as she served *kaffee* and treats. Every time she passed by him, she touched him in some way. A press of her hand against his shoulder. A touch on his wrist. Their fingers tangled when she handed him a mug of hot *kaffee*.

He was glad for her warm, steady presence. He couldn't wait to get her alone. They needed to talk. But the interruption wasn't completely unwelcome. The Barretts were kind and curious, and he didn't know what was going to happen after this, but he did know he was glad to open the lines of communication with them.

Ruby and Kimberly were sitting on a sofa across the room, Maggie on his wife's lap. Henry seemed to have zoned out of the conversations, standing near the window and staring outside. On the other side of the room, Todd and Michael were very interested in the details of David's job, how he learned his craft and what he loved about it.

David lost track of the conversation for a moment when he heard Kimberly say to Ruby, "You and David seem to be a perfect match."

Ruby felt David's eyes on her as Kimberly spoke the words. She let their gazes meet, smiled a wry smile for him because of the words the older woman had used.

"I don't know if anyone is ever a perfect match," Ruby said quietly. "But David is a *goot* husband and partner, and I am grateful he's in my life."

David's eyes narrowed slightly, but Michael spoke to him, and he was forced to stop listening to Ruby's conversation.

I love you. She'd almost said the words earlier, when David had come to meet her at the buggy, when the Barretts' car had pulled into the drive and she'd impulsively offered him support.

It was better if she didn't say it. She could show him every day in a hundred little ways. David might not ever get over the grief of losing Jessica. And this way, Ruby wasn't pressuring him to say the words back. There was no expectation from her, only the love she planned to give to him.

It was better this way.

"Maaaamm!" Maggie's plaintive wail and pushed-out bottom lip were all Ruby needed to see to know the girl was ready for her nap. Ruby went to her and scooped her up off the floor.

Mindy didn't need a nap every day, but today she was blinking blearily from her spot next to David on the couch. Obviously the excitement of having company now and that of playing with her cousins earlier had tired her out.

"Mindy, come help me tuck Maggie in for her nap," Ruby coaxed.

By the time she'd laid Maggie down and convinced Mindy to rest for a little bit, and then returned downstairs, the Barretts were donning their jackets and saying goodbyes.

Kimberly pressed Ruby's hands between hers. "Would it be all right if I wrote to you? It's been a long time since I've written a letter instead of using my computer."

"Of course." Kimberly was easy to like. It wouldn't be a challenge to write to her. Ruby could have the girls draw pictures, and she'd send those, too.

David shook Michael's hand. "When my *mamm* is feeling better, I'll ask if she and *daed* would think about getting together, all of us. She has all the best stories from when I was a child."

Michael and Kimberly smiled through new tears.

"We'd like that," Michael said.

Ruby caught sight of Henry, standing slightly behind his father, as he stared down at his feet, a muscle in his cheek jumping. The younger brother hadn't said much today, mostly listened. The frown he wore now hinted at unhappiness.

But she didn't have time to wonder more, because they were taking their leave. Kimberly couldn't contain the tears that spilled over when David hugged her goodbye. She sniffled into a tissue as her husband ushered her out to the car.

Ruby stood on the porch watching, David next to her, as they drove away. She shivered. A cold front must've blown in while they'd been inside. The pleasant sunshine from the afternoon was blocked by gray clouds skating across the sky.

She jumped when David's arm dropped around her shoulders. His hand rubbed her upper arm as he shared his warmth with her.

"We'd better get you inside before you turn into an icicle."

His warm, affectionate smile made her stomach dip, and she ducked her head to scurry inside, heart beating in her ears.

She picked up the coffee mugs that had been left haphazardly across the room and went into the kitchen, where the kitten they'd named Sue was batting a dust bunny beneath the table.

David followed Ruby. "I'll wash if you want to dry."

Her heart was still clamoring after his devastating smile from the front porch, but she got out a clean towel from one of the drawers as he filled the sink with soapy water.

"I like them—the Barretts," he said as he dunked the empty coffee mugs beneath the water. He didn't seem in any hurry as he turned his head in her direction, his gaze easy and curious. "What do you think?"

What did she think? She thought they'd done dishes together a few times, usually after the girls had gone to bed for the night, and none of those times felt like this.

There was something different about David. It was a tension missing from his shoulders, maybe, or the way his body seemed to turn toward hers without actually moving.

She felt flustered, and her cheeks were hot. "I

like them, too. Kimberly seemed taken with the girls. Todd is certainly talkative."

"Mmm. You'll never guess who else was talkative today." He handed her a clean mug, tugging gently against her hold until her eyes met his. His eyes were dancing in a teasing way.

"Who?" Was that her voice, breathless and barely there?

"My *daed*."

"Really?"

"Really." He finished washing up the mugs, handing each one off to her as he told her how they'd cleared the air, how his *daed* had guessed about the baby switch and been so afraid for all these years. How they'd made a tentative sort of peace.

She held the last mug between her hands, wiping it with the last dry corner of the towel. "I'm glad for you. It's wonderful *goot* that you have two families who love you." *And me.*

She swallowed the words that wanted to escape. It was only because David was close, because of the way he'd been smiling at her before. That's why the words she didn't want to say were so close to the surface. She turned her shoulder slightly as she put the last mug on the drying rack on the counter.

The sink *glugged* as it drained. From her peripheral vision, she saw him drying his hands with a towel. Maybe if she focused on something else, the urge to tell him would subside.

"There were a lot of leftovers from supper last night. I can reheat them when the girls wake up." Dinner was a safe conversation.

But David was right there, tugging on the edge of her apron skirt. "Supper can wait. There's something I need to say to you."

She glanced up as his hand cupped her elbow. His expression was serious and intense as he stared down into her eyes.

"I realized something, when I was talking with my *daed*. I was acting just like him."

She shook her head slightly, not breaking eye contact. She didn't understand.

"He spent all those years holding me at arm's length because he was scared. When I was about ten, I promised myself I would never turn out like him. But when Jessica died, I shut down. I was frightened to love someone again. I was doing the same thing to you that my *daed* had done to me."

Oh.

Her heart was pounding in her ears again, threatening to drown out his words.

"And you came into our lives and…"

Her heart fell to her toes at his hesitation. "We agreed this marriage was a friendship," she said gently, while her heart longed to blurt out her feelings for him.

He shook his head, his eyes warm. "That's not *goot* enough for me. Not anymore."

What was he saying?

"You are so easy to love," he said.

What?

She hadn't even realized she'd lowered her gaze until the fingers of his opposite hand came to nudge her chin upward.

It was there in the warmth of his gaze, only she'd been too scared herself to see it for what it was.

"I've been falling for you from the start, Ruby," he said softly. "I love you. And I don't want to hide from it—or from you—anymore."

"I love you, too."

He released a breath, some tension leaving him. "Then these are happy tears?"

She hadn't even realized she was crying.

She nodded as both of his hands came up to brush away her tears.

His eyes were a little misty, too. "I heard what you said earlier. Maybe we aren't a perfect match. But we are a *goot* match."

He kissed her gently as joy overflowed. Touched his forehead to hers. "A very *goot* match."

Chapter Twenty-Two

"They're here! *Mamm*, they're here!"

Mindy's muffled exclamation from the living room was punctuated by Maggie's *"Mamm! Mamm!"* and the banging of her wooden spoon on the kitchen floor.

Mindy raced in from the living room waving her arms wildly. "They're here!" she gasped.

Ruby took a slow step toward the doorway and could see from the wide living room windows that a gray sports car was coming up the drive.

"I see," she told Mindy, who stopped only to scratch Sue's head beneath the table before darting back into the living room to stand at the window.

David's brothers were coming for a visit on this blustery December Saturday.

The back door opened, and a cold wind blew in with Ruby's husband.

"Looks like it might snow," he said by way of a greeting. He came to her, straight as an arrow, and nuzzled his face against her jaw, making her jump.

"You're cold!" she exclaimed as the shock of his chilled skin registered. She pushed him away with a laugh. "And your brothers are here."

He cooed at Maggie on the floor and went to the sink to wash up. "You're still working on the bread?"

There was only curiosity in his tone.

"I sat down for a bit earlier. It'll get finished eventually."

She'd offered to make several loaves of fresh bread to help Beth. She and Evan were hosting house church tomorrow, and Beth was still fighting awful morning sickness. Which Ruby was now even more sympathetic about.

"*Goot.* I'm glad you took some rest. You work too hard." David shook the excess water off his hands and reached for the towel as he tried to see through the living room doorway.

"Go greet your brothers," she said, happy for him to go into the living room.

He brushed a kiss on her cheek and went out, not noticing anything amiss.

You work too hard.

Not today. She'd been so sleepy after lunchtime, and David had been working at the forge.

She'd set the girls with a coloring book in the living room and sat down in the rocking chair to catch her breath. She must've dozed off, because she'd woken with a start at one of Maggie's happy shrieks as she'd played with her sister.

The exhaustion, plus the bouts of nausea over the past several mornings had confirmed what she'd started suspecting last week. Lily had had similar symptoms at the beginning of both of her pregnancies.

She kneaded the dough on the flour-covered counter, each motion rolling along with her thoughts.

She *might* be pregnant.

But she wasn't sure.

She wished for her *mamm*. Wished she could be here so Ruby could ask her advice. *Mamm* would know.

But *Mamm* wasn't here. And Ruby wasn't ready to tell David. Not until she was sure.

Or at least, not at this moment, when his brothers were coming to visit.

Todd and David's parents had visited Hickory Harbor numerous times over the past months. It had been a slow process of getting to know each other. Sometimes awkward as David and his *Englisher* family navigated the tentative new relationship. Amos and Leah had been a part of some of the get-togethers, sharing about David when he'd been an infant and small child.

Things weren't perfect, but she'd stopped expecting perfection. Things were *goot*. Very *goot*.

She heard the commotion in the living room that meant David's brothers were here. But it was only Todd who peeked his head in the kitchen doorway. "Hello, Ruby."

"Hi, Todd. Where's Henry?"

Some shadow passed behind his eyes, but his smile didn't waver. "He had some work to finish up."

Something told her that wasn't the whole truth, but she didn't press him on it.

"Looks like you're busy, too," Todd teased.

"Not too busy to make you cinnamon rolls yesterday. I'll finish up here and bring some out."

He groaned in appreciation. "I love you, you know."

"She's taken," David growled good-naturedly from just behind him.

Ruby laughed.

David pushed past Todd and crossed the kitchen, calling over his shoulder, *"Kaffee?"*

"I never say no to coffee. Thanks."

Todd settled his shoulder against the doorjamb.

Ruby was thankful he felt at home here. David needed his brothers.

The pot was still on the stove, just out of Ruby's reach, where she was working the dough into a ball to be scooped into the bowl she had waiting so it could spend some time rising.

David stood nearby, pouring Todd's *kaffee* into a mug. Ruby got a strong waft of the bitter scent, and all of a sudden her stomach was roiling. She tried to breathe out, but the scent seemed to be glued to the insides of her nostrils.

"What's wrong?" David watched her closely, and she realized she'd pressed one hand to her tumbling stomach.

She shook her head, not sure it was safe to try and speak.

"Let her sit down," Todd said. When had he come into the room? He pulled out a chair from the table.

David put one hand under her elbow and helped her cross the room, but he'd somehow kept the cup in his other hand.

He set it on the table as he guided her into the chair, and some of the brown liquid sloshed over the side of the mug. The scent grew even stronger, and Ruby's nausea grew with it.

She turned her head, closing her eyes as she tried to breathe through her mouth, breathe through the thought of getting sick.

When she opened her eyes, Todd was squatting in front of her. David was sitting in the closest chair, his hand closed over her clammy one on the table.

"Why didn't you tell me you had an upset stomach?" David chided gently.

"I don't. I mean—it'll go away in a minute."

Todd watched her with knowing eyes. "Any other symptoms?"

She didn't want to tell him, didn't want David to find out like this. But with her husband watching her with intense concern, she had no choice.

"Tiredness." Todd didn't blink. Somehow he knew, just from one look at her. He had a *goot* bedside manner. "Mood swings?"

She nodded slowly.

"Anything else?"

She didn't want to say it aloud, didn't want to talk about her time of the month with him. She nodded instead.

A slow smile spread across his lips, one that reminded her of her husband. "Congratulations."

She looked at David, who wore a puzzled expression. It was a little adorable that he could still be confused after being a father twice over.

"We're going to have a baby," she whispered. "I think. I was planning to see Doc Bradshaw, but…" But the elderly gentleman had suffered a medical emergency, and his practice had been closed since.

It took a moment for the words to sink in for

David. She saw the realization dawn, the joy unfold over his features. "Are you—" He glanced between her and Todd. "You think so, too?"

Todd shrugged. "I just walked in. Haven't even had my coffee yet. But the morning sickness isn't new, I'm guessing?"

She shook her head slowly while David's expression went back to concern. "Why didn't you say anything?"

"I wanted to be sure." And maybe she'd been a little hesitant. Would her news make him think of Jessica? The family they might've wanted but not had a chance to have? She hadn't known how to broach the subject without hurting him.

"A baby," he breathed out. When he leaned in for a joyous kiss, she heard Todd stand up and leave the room, calling for Mindy.

"This is a *goot* day," David murmured as he hugged her. "A very *goot* day."

David found himself in a state of pleasant, surprised shock every time he glanced at Ruby.

She kept catching him at it and sending him her secret smiles or sometimes waving off his concern.

A new baby to welcome.

There was a part of him that still couldn't believe it. He had thought about it before, of course. Thought about what it would mean to bring a new baby brother or sister for Mindy and Maggie. He wanted their family to grow.

Todd wore a bemused smile every time he caught David watching his wife. Thankfully, his brother didn't seem to mind David's distraction.

When Maggie got cranky, Ruby shooed David and Todd outside. David shrugged into his coat on the porch. He and Todd took a slow walk around the yard, not in a hurry to get anywhere, though Todd checked his fancy watch frequently.

"Maybe I should learn how to drive a buggy," Todd said as they passed by the barn.

"I can teach you."

"Only if you let me teach you how to drive my car." Over the last few months, David had noticed that Todd was proud of his fancy sports car.

David shook his head. He didn't need a fancy car to be happy. He loved his simple Amish life.

Todd glanced out at the road. "My residency is up next month. I'll be the newest ER doctor at Mount Vernon Grace Hospital."

"*Goot* for you."

Todd's mouth pulled, not quite a smile. "I probably won't have as much time to visit. New doctor gets the worst shifts."

Oh. David had loved getting to know his brother. The last thing he wanted was for them to grow apart.

And then there was Ruby's condition.

"Do you have to start right away?"

Todd glanced at him curiously. "Why do you ask?"

David rubbed the back of his neck. "Doc Bradshaw has been talking about retiring for at least a decade. None of us thought he'd ever go through with it. But he had a stroke, and now we don't have a doctor at all."

Todd wrinkled his brows. "The town will want to hire a family medicine doctor, not an ER doctor. You need Band-Aids and vaccinations, not emergency surgery," he explained when David must've looked confused.

David didn't understand all the medical terminology Todd used. He knew his brother had gone to school for almost ten years after high school graduation.

"We'll get one. It's a *goot* practice. Doc Bradshaw was always busy. But it could take months. Why couldn't you come here for a short time and help us through the transition?"

Todd passed a hand over his mouth, his stare off in the distance. "Why couldn't I?" he mumbled under his breath.

"And Ruby will need a doctor to check up on her." David said the words without looking at his brother.

"Aha! The real reason you brought it up." Todd nudged his arm.

David hadn't had enough time to think about Ruby's pregnancy. There was a myriad of things that could go wrong. He'd have to trust God and pray. But having a *goot* doctor like Todd here would help, too.

"Not the only reason. We missed out on building tree houses and riding bikes, but there are still things I'd like to do together. Take you fishing. Teach you to drive a buggy."

Todd was contemplating it. He hadn't refused outright.

"I don't know if my new bosses would push out my start date," he finally said. "But I'll think about it."

"Okay."

It would be a blessing to have Todd in town. He was kind and generous, and he doted on Mindy and Maggie. He had fallen into the role of uncle naturally.

Henry was another story. He'd only been to visit once and had been quiet and almost angry while David had spent time with his parents. David didn't know why, and when he tried to ask Todd about it, his older brother had only said that Henry would come around in time.

David felt a pang of regret for the relationship that might never be. But all he could do was keep reaching out to Henry. He sent him a letter once a month, telling him about his life and thoughts and asking some questions about Henry. So far, there had been no response.

"If it did work out, Mom and Dad would be jealous that I would get to see you and Ruby and the girls more. Maybe Mom could come down and stay with me for a few weeks."

It sounded wonderful. David's relationship with the Barretts had grown, though it still felt awkward at times. He enjoyed getting to know them. They didn't push for more than he was ready for. They seemed eager to learn about his life, and they were happy in theirs.

He and his *daed* had rebuilt a relationship that he'd long thought damaged beyond repair. His *daed* would never be the most talkative person in the world, but they had built a dresser together that now stood proudly in the empty room up-stairs. It would be Mindy's room soon, David realized. Maybe he would ask his *daed* whether they could make a bed for her. With everything out in the open, it was easier for *daed* to share his feelings, though he was still quiet by nature.

Mindy called out from the porch, and David realized that she and Ruby had put on coats and come outside. Maggie must be sleeping in the house.

Just in time for the snow to start falling. It came down from the sky in fluffy clumps. If it

Get 3 FREE REWARDS!

We'll send you 2 FREE Books plus a FREE Mystery Gift.

FREE Value Over **$20**

Both the **Harlequin® Special Edition** and **Harlequin® Heartwarming™** series feature compelling novels filled with stories of love and strength where the bonds of friendship, family and community unite.

YES! Please send me 2 FREE novels from the Harlequin Special Edition or Harlequin Heartwarming series and my FREE Gift (gift is worth about $10 retail). After receiving them, if I don't wish to receive any more books, I can return the shipping statement marked "cancel." If I don't cancel, I will receive 6 brand-new Harlequin Special Edition books every month and be billed just $5.49 each in the U.S. or $6.24 each in Canada, a savings of at least 12% off the cover price, or 4 brand-new Harlequin Heartwarming Larger-Print books every month and be billed just $6.24 each in the U.S. or $6.74 each in Canada, a savings of at least 19% off the cover price. It's quite a bargain! Shipping and handling is just 50¢ per book in the U.S. and $1.25 per book in Canada.* I understand that accepting the 2 free books and gift places me under no obligation to buy anything. I can always return a shipment and cancel at any time by calling the number below. The free books and gift are mine to keep no matter what I decide.

Choose one: ☐ **Harlequin Special Edition** (235/335 BPA GRMK) ☐ **Harlequin Heartwarming Larger-Print** (161/361 BPA GRMK) ☐ **Or Try Both!** (235/335 & 161/361 BPA GRPZ)

Name (please print)

Address | Apt. #

City | State/Province | Zip/Postal Code

Email: Please check this box ☐ if you would like to receive newsletters and promotional emails from Harlequin Enterprises ULC and its affiliates. You can unsubscribe anytime.

Mail to the Harlequin Reader Service:
IN U.S.A.: P.O. Box 1341, Buffalo, NY 14240-8531
IN CANADA: P.O. Box 603, Fort Erie, Ontario L2A 5X3

Want to try 2 free books from another series? Call 1-800-873-8635 or visit www.ReaderService.com.

Get 3 FREE REWARDS!

We'll send you 2 FREE Books plus a FREE Mystery Gift.

FREE Value Over **$20**

Both the **Love Inspired®** and **Love Inspired® Suspense** series feature compelling novels filled with inspirational romance, faith, forgiveness and hope.

YES! Please send me 2 FREE novels from the Love Inspired or Love Inspired Suspense series and my FREE gift (gift is worth about $10 retail). After receiving them, if I don't wish to receive any more books, I can return the shipping statement marked "cancel." If I don't cancel, I will receive 6 brand-new Love Inspired Larger-Print books or Love Inspired Suspense Larger-Print books every month and be billed just $6.49 each in the U.S. or $6.74 each in Canada. That is a savings of at least 16% off the cover price. It's quite a bargain! Shipping and handling is just 50¢ per book in the U.S. and $1.25 per book in Canada.* I understand that accepting the 2 free books and gift places me under no obligation to buy anything. I can always return a shipment and cancel at any time by calling the number below. The free books and gift are mine to keep no matter what I decide.

Choose one: ☐ **Love Inspired Larger-Print** (122/322 BPA GRPA)   ☐ **Love Inspired Suspense Larger-Print** (107/307 BPA GRPA)   ☐ **Or Try Both!** (122/322 & 107/307 BPA GRRP)

Name (please print)

Address   Apt. #

City   State/Province   Zip/Postal Code

Email: Please check this box ☐ if you would like to receive newsletters and promotional emails from Harlequin Enterprises ULC and its affiliates. You can unsubscribe anytime.

Mail to the Harlequin Reader Service:
IN U.S.A.: P.O. Box 1341, Buffalo, NY 14240-8531
IN CANADA: P.O. Box 603, Fort Erie, Ontario L2A 5X3

Want to try 2 free books from another series! Call 1-800-873-8635 or visit www.ReaderService.com.

---

*Terms and prices subject to change without notice. Prices do not include sales taxes, which will be charged (if applicable) based on your state or country of residence. Canadian residents will be charged applicable taxes. Offer not valid in Quebec. This offer is limited to one order per household. Books received may not be as shown. Not valid for current subscribers to the Love Inspired or Love Inspired Suspense series. All orders subject to approval. Credit or debit balances in a customer's account(s) may be offset by any other outstanding balance owed by or to the customer. Please allow 4 to 6 weeks for delivery. Offer available while quantities last.

Your Privacy—Your information is being collected by Harlequin Enterprises ULC, operating as Harlequin Reader Service. For a complete summary of the information we collect, how we use this information and to whom it is disclosed, please visit our privacy notice located at corporate.harlequin.com/privacy-notice. From time to time we may also exchange your personal information with reputable third parties. If you wish to opt out of this sharing of your personal information, please visit readerservice.com/consumerchoice or call 1-800-873-8635. **Notice to California Residents**—Under California law, you have specific rights to control and access your data. For more information on these rights and how to exercise them, visit corporate.harlequin.com/california-privacy.

LIRLIS23

HARLEQUIN
PLUS

Try the best multimedia subscription service for romance readers like you!

Read, Watch and Play.

Experience the easiest way to get the romance content you crave.

Start your **FREE TRIAL** at
www.harlequinplus.com/freetrial.

LICNM0623

Dear Reader,

Thank you for reading A Convenient Amish Bride. I loved getting to know the characters David and Ruby, and I hope you did, too. Community is so necessary, isn't it? Having a strong family, group of friends and church community around is so vitally important to our lives. David didn't have that because he was an only child and because he closed himself off (for a reason). And it's what Ruby brought back to his life. My community has changed me for the better, been there for me when I needed help, challenged me to be a better, more godly person. I hope and pray that you have a strong community (small or large!) around you. God bless and thank you for reading.

Lucy Bayer

kept up, it would be perfect for making a snow-man tomorrow.

Ruby stood at the porch railing. She smiled at him, and even from a distance, David saw the quiet joy she brought to every part of their lives.

He hadn't expected her, would never have pre-dicted what having her in his life would be like, but he wouldn't change any of it.

God was blessing them with a new member in their family, and he could think of no one he would rather share the blessing with.

* * * * *